A CHINESE SUMMER

A CHINESE
—
SUMMER

Mark Illis

To Saul,
Happy Birthday

BLOOMSBURY

First published 1988

Copyright © 1988 by Mark S. Illis

Bloomsbury Publishing Ltd, 2 Soho Square, London W1V 5DE

British Library Cataloguing in Publication Data
Illis, Mark S, 1963-
A Chinese summer.
I. Title
823′ .914[F]
ISBN 0-7475-0257-9

Printed in Great Britain by
Butler & Tanner Ltd, Frome and London

The summer lay before Simon like foreign territory – as if it were Chinese
and he didn't have the phrasebook. And where would he be once he'd
crossed it? Chinese walls kept other people strangely incommunicado. For
the present he was trying to regain the knack of being alone in the flat –
without Helen's make-up in the bathroom, without her irritating habits,
or her nice habits. It was as if she had taken him with her, the place was
that empty. What in the world did he do before he met her?

Then there was the accident – the idiom of the hospital to fathom:
secrets and codes, mouthed by strangers, pertaining to his body. There
was the danger of finding himself content in this clinical oasis of order,
though an elusive fear occasionally nudged him. No, he must get out,
break down the walls and learn to speak Chinese.

In a captivating début Mark Illis follows the chain of events that brings
a young man through crisis – emotional and physical. Every nuance of
Simon's curious perception of his experience that summer is brought
artfully and memorably to the page in a first novel of rich originality.

TO ALAN, JACQUI AND GINNI

SILENCE

This is the weekend after the end of the story.

I lay in the half-dark staring out of the window, brooding until I didn't know the difference between sleeping and waking. I floated weightless outside over the street always staring upwards, staring upwards as if trying to measure the distance. I dreamt that there was someone sitting at the end of my bed and I woke up shouting and chased them across the room; and then I stood there rubbing my eyes and turned on the light and looked behind the curtain, and sat down to play some patience.

I have a book in which there are twenty-seven varieties of the game. I shifted cards and turned them over, made little piles and patterns, gathered them up and shuffled them and began again. I pushed back the sheet and spread my legs wide and built a card-house on the mattress. It rose to a fragile eminence and then collapsed on its trembling foundation. I picked up the cards and started again.

In the morning, when I got out of bed, cards slid from the duvet to the floor and lay scattered, like a wayward Tarot reading. I found my suitcase in the cupboard in the hall, dropped it in the middle of the bedroom and started throwing things into it. Books, clothes, some tapes, the radio. I circled it, going round the room from shelf to drawer to desk, and threw things over my shoulder, under a leg, in short curving arcs and straightforward nose-dives. When it was full I put the rest of the essentials in a couple of plastic bags and went in to the kitchen for a cup of tea. There was no milk, so it was black and bitter. I sat at the small table and read a cookbook, sipping the drink and breaking the corners off a piece of cheese. I didn't look at the dirty plates in the sink and I didn't touch the rotting vegetables at the bottom of the fridge. Instead I considered chicken cooked with oranges and almonds.

Breakfast over, I went back to the bedroom, put on a jacket, found my keys and wallet and tried to pick up my case. Someone had nailed it to the floor. I picked up a plastic bag and watched the red lettering near my hand grow as the plastic stretched, 'Fruit' becoming 'FRuIT'. I dropped the bag, sat on the bed and stared at the suitcase. It stared me down.

The cards still lay on the floor, but I couldn't bring myself to use them. The idea of another game was degrading. So I left, driven out of my own bedroom by a piece of luggage and a pack of cards.

It was a bright late April day and it felt as if summer was starting early. I unzipped my jacket and rolled up the sleeves, feeling a welcome coolness on my chest. There was just enough breeze, not too much. The park was alive with primary colours and people were walking around with small, unconscious smiles on their faces. Roots were probably on the move under my feet. I sat down in the first big patch of green that I came to, sat down heavily and stared around aggressively, like a suitcase.

A bell rang, and minutes later the place was swarming with small boys in three-piece suits. Dark blue or black suits and little skullcaps. They were running around aimlessly, apparently for the sake of running, but one shouted Hey!
I'm going a different way
I'll meet you there
I'm going a different way,
like an impromptu poem, with a rhythm following his running feet. He set off purposefully in a different direction, clearly with a destination firmly in mind.

I watched movements and configurations around me, hoping to see some significant action. Two young, bearded men walked down the path beside the grass, their suits covered by long blue overcoats, their caps seeming to defy gravity. It was an odd uniform for this time of day and this weather, but, deep in conversation, they were unselfconscious, as if they and the boys were all involved in a complicated game which was out of bounds to others.

A change of focus. The grass was a part of everything, not a

2

background or a foreground but the stage on which the action was played, peopled by insects and the boys out of shul. It interfered with my perspective: grasshoppers were giants and the boys running away were gnats, incomprehensibly busy. The grass was a part of it all, a livid green, smelling of sex, pushing between my fingers, reaching up around my face as I lay on my stomach, touching my cheeks and nostrils. When I finally moved, I had almost to shrug it off, like a coat.

The playground was packed with children and their parents. Here was a way to spend time. There were colourful seesaws and swings, a slide next to an overflowing sandpit, a geodesic climbing frame and a roundabout as busy as a bus in the rush-hour. The hubbub of gleeful shouts and cries of excitement swung and swirled in the air. For a moment I recognized in myself the sickening sensation of being a reluctant outsider, forced to become a spectator. The moment came and went, elusive like all my sensations at that time. Snapshots passed from hand to hand. Leaning on the railing which surrounded the area I watched a young mother approaching, pushing a pram with one hand and holding on to a small boy with the other. I held the gate open for her and she gave me a harrassed smile. The boy looked up at me curiously. I winked and he let out a surprising whoop and looked away immediately, bashfully burying his face in his mother's dress, while at the same time his free hand flapped wildly above his head. Then he ran for it, followed more sedately by his mother. He threw me another look from the sanctuary of the sandpit, and literally fell over backwards when he saw that I was still watching him. When he sat up he had his hands over his eyes and was peering at me through a chink between his fingers. This was safe apparently. We looked at each other steadily, and his lips began to move with a silent message, possibly words of encouragement addressed to himself, or an invitation to me to join him.

On the way back to my flat I tried conscientiously to leave self-pity behind me in the park, but it wouldn't be left. It was as insistent as a sexual fantasy, temporarily displaced only to return stronger than ever. What in the world did I do before I met her? How did I spend my days? I had lost the knack of being alone.

3

Inside, it was the stillness that scared me. There was already an air of permanence in the quietness, as if I had moved in alone and was renting the place for myself.

I moved the tv from the kitchen into my bedroom and turned it on. Sat in front of it. Made myself comfortable. I watched it all afternoon and evening, and well into the night sitting on the bed sinking into the duvet with my back to the window and my feet on the suitcase. Behind me the low sound of the traffic finding its way through the glass; in front, a diahorrea of images. When it got very bad I turned the sound down and dubbed my own dialogue. I feel like an explorer back from a remote country, spreading the word to the stay-at-home types: it is possible to explore your tv to that extent, ending up with nothing worse than a slight hangover the next day.

I turned round at some point in the late afternoon and found myself looking at a sheep. We gazed at each other politely, and I realised that there was a whole two-tiered lorry-load of sheep outside, packed in like slaves, waiting for the lights to change.

Later I thought about the recipe I had looked at, but, although I could almost smell its flavour, I couldn't be bothered to make it.

When I eventually left my corner for fifteen minutes I found that the autobank was rejecting my card in any case, so I settled for some more cheese, with prawn crackers from the take-away.

At four in the morning the sky was non-committal and quiet, steel blue along its edge, but still grey. The lights changed on the empty road as if talking to themselves. They were unusually bright. The dark windows across the road stared back at me implacably.

'Simon,' she said, yet again, 'this isn't working any more. I'm leaving tonight.'

'Well shit,' I answered, 'give me another chance. I'll use more chili next time.'

She started to cry, which I thought must be a good sign, but when I got up to hug her she rose too and ran out of the kitchen. I stood there stupidly for a moment, and then she was in the hall, carrying her suitcase.

'I packed it this afternoon,' she explained.

'Helen . . .'

'I'll be in touch.'

I slept eventually, and woke late in a tangle of sheets and duvet. I wondered whether I wanted a newspaper but, looking out of the window, I saw that the shop was already shut. I found out the times of some trains I could catch from a gloomy British Rail recording, and I put on the hot water for a bath. Emotional crises in my life go hand in hand with malnutrition and hygiene.

While it was getting hot I considered lunch. I went into the kitchen and had a look around, thinking of Sunday lunch at home, Steve carving, Sammy making a nuisance of himself and Dad rattling on religiously. I moved some things around: all the cutlery went into the sink and all the envelopes, corks, rubber bands and fuses went into the cutlery drawer. I had a glass of water, and then a lukewarm bath. I lay deep in it, so that the water lapped at my temples and forehead, and I listened to it breathe. I dozed for a while, floating, then I sneezed myself awake and hit my head on the enamel.

Fluff from the carpet stuck to my wet feet as I took some clean clothes out of the suitcase. I put the dirty clothes into another plastic bag and redistributed some of my possessions. I picked up the FRuIT bag again, and it became FRUIT, only with the 'F' more capital than the rest, to even things out.

I still hadn't made a decision, but I had begun to think about the consequences of moving. I wasn't ready to go home to my parents and my younger brother. I hadn't spoken a word since Friday evening and, so far, silence suited me. All my belongings were neatly packed now, waiting. Let them wait.

They were playing cricket. I sat on a bench between the pitch and the playground listening to the squeak and whine of the swings behind me. Why is there nowhere *good* to go? The question had become lodged in my mind, the word 'good' stretching to match the drawn-out sound of the swings. Nowhere good to go. That was probably at the heart of the problem. Why was there nowhere good? The white and creamy figures advanced and retreated. The bat swung as the invisible ball approached . . . there was the occasional resonant thud followed by running. Sometimes some applause. On the boundary two boys were playing their own version of the game.

People were walking their dogs or their youngest children, talking in fragments over their heads.
It could be that he never knew
Because he came from Israel
He spoilt his chance and never knew
Because he came from Israel.
It was a question of interpretation: I imagined an immigrant, bearded and bewildered, his future blighted through lack of adaptation to some eccentric English custom. The light was bad now, but the game proceeded at a luxurious pace.

'I'm falling down.'

The girl's voice fell through her words and toyed with tears but decided against them. After all she wasn't going to fall down, she was cycling between her parents on a noisy little bike with stabilisers. Her parents were like stabilisers themselves. A small white dog ran towards her and, sure enough, her mother reached out to steady her as it ran between them. The dog stopped abruptly and stood in the middle of the path, panting slightly. Lost, it looked around, surprisingly human. It ran after a big alsatian which ignored it entirely, much more interested in people. Still it ran after the bigger dog, snapping at its heels, hoping for attention. The owner of the alsatian snarled as he saw me. 'Training.' He was a small, stooped man whose eyes were lost in wrinkles, and his voice, like my thoughts, matched the squeak and whine of the swings. I shook my head, unsettled by his malevolent glare, to indicate that the white dog was not mine. He walked on, and I watched him until he was out of sight behind the trees.

The ball bounced across the boundary. Someone had misfielded, and his hands clutched his head as he fell over into the consolation of the grass. Now one of the boys playing bat and ball dropped a catch. He shook the hand the ball fell out of, as if he was angry with its clumsiness.

The creamy-coloured cricketers were turning to grey. A man on the boundary threw the ball into the air towards the wicket, his arm moving in dreamy slow motion, and the ball was swallowed by the gloom, to become invisible again.

The suitcase was ajar, grinning at me. I picked it up and emptied it onto the floor. There were plans to be made, I needed to organise my days, discipline them. Methodically I gathered the fallen cards, replaced my possessions in drawers and on shelves, put the suitcase back in its cupboard, and then began to think about Monday, and about Mondays in general.

JUNE

THE SMALLPOX
EMPORIUM

I had an elaborate fantasy.

She is lying beneath a thin sheet, her eyes closed, the lashes like feathers. The in-curving slope of her throat glides down to her collarbone. Her breasts smoothly rise to the lip of the sheet. The cotton stirs as she breathes. I love her more than ever, the bitch.

There is a junk shop in Kentish Town which is caked in dust and washed in bleached yellow light, like an old sepia print. It is narrow, and it stretches back into increasing gloom like a cave. The owner is a hunched goblin, with a large round face wizened like a walnut. Eyes lost in wrinkles. When the door opens, he snarls. Lurking behind his wares, he watches his customers browse, and snorts indignantly if they seem to be taking too long. When a person is leaving without having bought anything, he will sometimes take them by the arm – or the wrist, which is more easily reached – and accompany them out of the shop, abusing them viciously in a polite, friendly manner. When he has closed the door behind them he capers around his limited floor-space, obviously delighted that he has not parted with any of his possessions. He may at such times lift a ratty, moulding volume from his shelves, open it at random, and smell it rapturously; or he may seize a flea-bitten stuffed animal and embrace its decaying face as if it were a fluffy teddy-bear and he an affectionate child. His name is Mr Pock, and his shop is Pock's Emporium, known to one and all – partly because of its history as a ward in a long defunct Victorian hospital, and partly because of its present nature – known to one and all as the Smallpox Emporium.

I went in there one day on an impulse and, on another impulse, I bought a swordstick and an elephant's foot to keep it in. Mr Pock snatched my money from me with such a malevolent glare that I thought he might snatch the stick too, and use it on me. It is not sensible to aggravate Mr Pock. He bears grudges. Beads of sweat nestled in the folds of his skin and hung from his jowls. His face was scarlet now, changing in character to that of a wrinkled cherry left to fester. He looked, not just grotesque, but also horribly ill, and I wondered if germs still lingered in the quiet darkness with the aging junk.

The impulses must have been born from a well-defined subconscious intent, because events followed in an effortless sequence. It was a small foot – probably from a baby elephant – and very dirty, with an engrained dirt that I couldn't remove. I polished the toenails to a sickly yellow. The swordstick, beneath the dust, was of warm shining ebony, laced in silver from top to bottom, and broodingly sinister. I spent a day sharpening the blade, and polishing the wood and the silver. I would kill her neatly, like a surgeon. The style is the thing. The join was invisible, and when I drew the blade it flashed and sliced the gasping air, becoming an extension of my arm.

While she slept I held it above her, my legs apart and my right arm crooked back, sighting down the sword like a bullfighter, on tiptoe, poised absolutely still. She was naked on this warm June night. The tip of the blade lifted the sheet and carried it down to her waist, where it lay in rumpled folds. The obligatory pause. If only she wouldn't move. Her auburn hair fell away from her face; her smile did not reproach me. I should kiss her, and she should pray. If I knew she wouldn't move, it would be different. We would remain a motionless tableau, and I would always love her more than ever.

I lowered the blade. Touched her skin beneath her left rising and falling breast. . . Holding the moment, holding the moment, holding it . . . A globe of blood. A world of significance there if I could read it. I felt I could see my future mapped out there, clotting into something fixed and unalterable. She stirred; I knew she would. I was still in control, there was no crude thrust; the style is the thing. I slid it in smoothly beneath her ribcage. No resistance. She sighed, and then she was dead.

12

I was drained. Should I have kissed her then? I wiped the blade clean on her stomach, there was hardly any blood from such a tidy wound, and I walked home. I limped a little. People looked at me sympathetically.

Why am I limping? At this point I am always limping home with my dandy's cane, it is after the murder, and people mistake my demeanour.

Next, the body. I drove back the next morning and airily let myself in to her flat. One more look. Now she was pale, as pale as her sheets. The aftermath was always messy and less interesting. I lifted her and she bled again, making the linen dirty. She was heavy, much heavier than I expected. Her head hung back as if she couldn't bear to look at me. The details were always the same. The blood spreading like a four-leaf clover.

I maintained decorum in the face of her crudity, dressing her lovingly and with care. Lingerie, a sensible skirt and blouse. I dragged her in her bloody sheet-shroud to the door. My car was right outside, but it had been clamped. Hers then, further down the road. My hand caressed her hip as I found her keys. She drives a small bright-red Mini. I carried her across the pavement, half dragging her as if she was drunk; I laughed and smiled expressively at a man who passed: What can one do? He took a second look. I kissed her. That was when I kissed her, when she was no longer attractive. She leant on me as I opened the door. I sat her in the passenger seat. Clunk click.

She was smiling her baffling smile, an enigmatic mix of love and indifference. Her eyes were bright and there was a charming timidity about her. For a moment I just watched her, unable to start the car. As I watched, her expression slumped in a startling shift which revealed the dead solidity of her face. I became aware of a foul smell. I remembered the body I had dressed minutes earlier. A metamorphosis was happening as I sat there. We moved away, towards the canal.

A tall figure all in black steps on to the road, into my path, and hails me. A look on his face as if it's me, in particular, that he has been waiting for. He points to an area that has been set apart where chosen cars are being checked. A road-block? Already? My first thought is to speed away – a high-speed chase through the city and up the motorway like Burt Reynolds running moonshine, trailing wrecked cars and wailing sirens through the country. My second thought is to stop. They are only checking road-tax.

'Now then sir, this needs renewing.'

The face fills my window, the mouth is opening and shutting in slow-motion. I am still in control. I apologise, claim I forgot, look meek.

'Is the girl all right sir?'

I have to suppress an urge to laugh. She stinks, she sneers stupidly. She's tired and has had too much to drink and it's really nothing to worry about. I'm taking her home. She was drinking all night. Not me. I grin stupidly.

He looks at each of us. I think he wants to worm through the window and feel the pulse in her throat. He would pull his hand away and see the marks of his fingers left there, as if imprinted on wax. I can feel his breath on my cheek. The window is blocked. The car is so small.

'Can I have a look in the boot please sir?'

The boot? Of course. The shroud is in the boot. I get out of the car and I am almost glad because there is so much air now. I feel I may take steps into the air, up an invisible staircase. Someone stops him as we walk around the car. No time, he says, a lot to do today, just check the documents. He hesitates, and then turns round. I walk back down the staircase. It's going to be all right now. The documents are in the glove compartment. I open the passenger door and she falls sideways and hangs against the seatbelt, her head sinking towards the pavement as she slides under the strap and her eyelids falling open as her mouth falls shut, dribbling words through closed lips:

Simon, you fucked up *again*.

She always made an exhibition of herself in the end.

14

ANOTHER VOICE

The sun was probing through the crack in the curtains, and as I pulled them back it eagerly swarmed over me, and we got to know each other like new lovers. I rolled on the mattress, loving its warmth on my skin, feeling my inertia being gradually squeezed out of me by an impatient tide of energy. June was two weeks old, time was passing, and nothing happening and 'Where will you be,' I said suddenly, 'where will you be at this rate at the end of the summer? Still lying here, still wallowing here in bitterness?'

I sat up, my words, embarrassingly loud in the quiet room, becoming thoughts: There's no excuse, there's no excuse for not knowing what to do. For years there's been only one way to mark the beginning of summer: it is the season for going home.

The view from the window was a reflection of my state of mind and body over the past few weeks: shops shut, an empty pavement, one car at the lights, murmuring to itself. As I watched, the engine stuttered and the car moved slowly away. Sunday then, and everyone indoors. A day ahead . . . Quite abruptly, as if it had been there all along and I had only just noticed, I recognized in myself a craving for a sense of purpose. My elaborate fantasy, continually rerun, had me trapped like ruthless geometry. In its unchanging pattern I was cast as the villain, but I had actually shrunk to some lower status. A villain at least has a vigorous sense of himself, that was more than I could claim.

I swung my legs off the bed, sat now on the edge of the mattress, still not ready to stand up. What I need, I was thinking, is a framework. At home . . . the predictable rituals at home are what I need. 'So how's the job-hunting going?' Dad would say, raring to start another vicarious career. And I would prevaricate. He would be astonished if I did anything else.

15

Finally getting up, I went into the hall. On the floor by the door the receiver of the phone lay off the hook next to a small pile of unopened letters. I'd been incommunicado for a while. Islanded. Time for a change. I pulled the phone the length of its flex, so that I could stay in the sunlight. I paused. 'I am the son now,' I said. Silence doesn't suit me, and the fantasy doesn't represent my voice. That was wooden limbs and a painted grin operated by a hand slipped up the back. I am the son now.

I dialled the number and listened to the patient rings.

The sun grew less sure of itself as it climbed, but an uncertain shadow followed me to the bus-stop and waited with me there. I took the bus to the tube, the tube to the train, and the train to my home station. I had my suitcase with me, although to my mother I had only mentioned lunch. It would be a nice surprise. I hoped it would be a nice surprise; there had been a nervous quality in her voice over the phone, suggesting that there was something she was hesitating to tell me.

The tube seemed louder because it was empty, reverberations echoing in its frame as if it was a monstrous musical instrument. It rattled and slithered to a surprising halt in the middle of a tunnel. The carriages quietly hummed to each other. I got up and fingered the closed doors, peering through the glass, seeing only my reflection. Sitting down again I glanced up to find Helen opposite me, her small mouth pursed in exasperation. She wore a V-necked cotton top, and bright baggy trousers. Her hair was pulled away from her face, and tied in the ponytail she preferred. Her pale face bare.

'What are they *like* though?' she said.

'What do you mean 'what are they like'? They're like parents. Dad's always preaching about something, mum's always nagging. You know.'

'You're not trying to understand. How will you feel when you meet *my* parents? Won't you be a little bit curious, or apprehensive, or anything at all?'

Helen charmed me by worrying about unexpected things. She would worry about the impression she made on strangers she was

16

only likely to meet once. When she had a tutor she liked at college she would worry about her handwriting, and what she wore for tutorials. And she worried about meeting my parents.

'Don't worry,' I said, 'you'll be a hit with them.'

She laughed. 'Don't be silly.'

I'm not being silly, you *were* a hit with them. Almost embarrassingly so.

She made them laugh and she made them like her, to the extent that I could catch myself feeling jealous of her ease with them. I remembered watching fascinated as she met Steve, and his habitual prejudice against students dissolved in the face of her unassuming friendliness.

I would have to get in touch with Steve.

She still looked unconvinced. I wanted to sit beside her and put an arm around her.

'Just don't worry about it. *E*verybody likes you.'

She laughed again, it was an old joke between us. Her hand cupped her chin in a slightly nervous gesture, as if she was hiding excess flesh there.

The train jerked away with a peculiar grunt, and I saw my startled face in the window opposite. Up and down the carriage the light defined the emptiness. Everything was foreign now, needing a second look. Even the noises of the wheels and of the rushing air were worth listening to for ulterior meanings.

The local station only has two platforms, each covered by an arched, gappy roof which lets the rain in. There is a little wooden sign which tells you where the next train is going, and there are posters of Kent and Scotland, and adverts for the local hotel. None of it changes, it just gradually decays. Another pane of glass is broken, the paint peels off a little more, another poster is torn or defaced. A smoking golfball of a nuclear power station appears in the Kent countryside, and a woman advertising the Highlands finds herself menaced by a huge disembodied cock.

Not any more. The woman's predicament was finally over, because the posters were now encased in perspex, linked by thick tubes of shatter-proof red plastic. Red metal benches had grown beneath the restored awning. A new sign with a flashy logo welcomed the traveller to British Rail Network Southeast. Everything was clean and new, and determined to stay that way. I was uncomfortable. I felt some nostalgia for graffiti and dilapidation, but it was more than that. I felt that a bad precedent was being set, because sometimes I can tell the future, I *know* when things are going to go badly.

I walked home in steady sunlight, out of the village and on to the heath. I passed the church beside the still pond and arrived outside the school with the oak tree in the playground. I stared in where I used to stare out. An empty, surprisingly small stretch of concrete, faded yellow markings. I remembered heathen end-of-term assemblies at which hundreds of children would watch a multi-coloured summer shining through the stained glass, and would wait for the bell which meant that the holiday had started. Summer, season for going home. God was the organ, heavy and plodding, slowing down time, and the headmaster, distant and dull.

My memories were fine – they were poignant and vivid, it was the present that confused me. Green bins had sprouted on every corner, and one, which had mysteriously melted, was reduced to a frozen, bubbling monster, apparently hauling itself out of a drain. There were black plastic sacks outside every house, lumpy and tightly knotted, as if whole roadfuls of people had corpses to dispose of.

At home everything was covered in newspaper. My father was reading a newspaper in an armchair draped in a dustsheet in a huddle of hidden furniture.

He looked up as I came in, waving a tabloid at me and firing short sentences like bulletins. ' "Jack-in-Box Cops Kill Kids". What do you think of that? Illiterate, some of these boys. It's all fallen apart since I left. Where have you sprung from?'

A redundant printer, not a journalist, he felt his departure had been a symptom of a general decline in standards.

'Hello dad.' The room was unrecognizable. The smell was chemical and the old, warm beige on the walls was succumbing to bright new white. 'It's going to be nice,' I said.

'Don't give me that. It's a big mistake. Big mistake. I've tried, God knows I've tried, if you'll excuse the expression, but your mother won't listen.' He imitated her voice, pinching his heartiness into a fussy falsetto. 'The house has to be nice to come back to. I don't want to come back to a disaster area.' He smiled cheerfully. 'And she's in charge these days, you know. She wears the trousers. How are you anyway? Bless you.'

I hadn't sneezed – 'Bless you' is my father's favourite expression. Hearing it was like catching sight of an old friend in a crowd of strangers. He told everyone that it was only when he lost his job, on the same January day that my mother was promoted, that he had begun to blossom. It had all happened in my absence, and with the seasons we had grown apart. Before there had been efforts at least to speak to each other. Now there was heartiness, and good humour, and nothing was ever said.

I left him 'keeping an eye on lunch' and went into the garden to find my mother. She was sunbathing topless, lying very still with her arms stretched out and her fingers splayed in the grass. A long fingernail was probing the dry earth.

I watched her until she felt my presence and lifted herself on one elbow to look at me.

'I'm home,' I said. 'I'd like to stay for a while.'

She smiled, and crow's feet appeared as her eyes adjusted to the light. 'There you are. How are you?'

I was fine, so was she. I sat down and looked at the towel and the discarded sunglasses. The weather was warm but still indecisive, not yet committing itself.

'It's a bit early for sunbathing isn't it?'

'I'm getting acclimatized,' she said. 'We're flying next week.'

'Flying?'

'We're all going to stay with Steven in Malawi. Didn't you get my letter?'

'All of us? You're joking. We're going next week?'

Her face changed. 'I'm sorry Simon, I should have said all three of us.' She reached out to touch my face, and then seemed to think better of it. 'You know we can't really leave Sam with anyone here. And we can't afford four. Didn't you get my letter? I thought you'd be looking for jobs. I sent you a letter weeks ago, you mean it never arrived?'

19

'I haven't seen it.' I couldn't meet her eyes. 'Next week?'

She nodded. 'We'll be away for the summer. I'm having a sort of sabbatical.'

The indecisive sun found its way behind a cloud.

'I bet it's sunny there.'

'I understand it's the dry season. I think the days are very, very long. You know if you were really keen we could . . .'

'No, no,' I said, 'you're right. Of course you're right, I should be looking for jobs a bit harder. I sent some letters.'

My mother put her bikini on, reaching her arms behind her back as she stood up, looking as if she was rising on small, angular wings.

'I tried to get in touch,' she said. 'I kept hoping *you* would. Shall we go inside then?'

'I'll follow you. I've been indoors too long.'

I watched her go in, and then I lay back on her towel and closed my eyes. Fly away then, I was thinking, I don't need you. Lying in the impression her body had made, I could smell her. It was an irresistibly evocative smell, making me a child again. Fly away then, I thought, my hands grasping at the towel as if it was about to fly from under me.

I opened my eyes to find my little brother looking down at me with an air of studied indifference. At seven, he was trying to look twice his age. The sleeves of his t-shirt were rolled up, revealing a red lump on his left shoulder. His hands were in his pockets and he was chewing rhythmically. As I watched he gritted his teeth and pulled a wilting string of gum out of his mouth, to arm's length. (Not very far.) When he was satisfied that I had had a full viewing, he rolled it all up again and put it back.

'Look,' he said, pointing at the lump. 'My jab. I didn't cry.'

'Jab?'

'My cholera jab. The doctor said it wouldn't hurt but it did. You're lucky you're not having one. Where have you been anyway, all this time?' It sounded like an accusation.

'In the flat. How are you?'

'I'm going to Malawi.'

'I know.'

'Where's Helen?'

'I don't know that.'

'Haven't you seen her?'

'It's a long story. I don't want to talk about it, Sam.'

'Mum said you wouldn't.' He imitated my mother's voice, pushing his own high voice an octave higher. Sam, like my father, sometimes treated communication as a performance art. 'She said, "Don't ask Simon about Helen, they've had a row." What did you row about? Why is it a long story?'

'It's very hard for me to explain, Sam.' I winced at the words, terrified of patronising him.

We went inside together, to find that our parents had made lunch. Newspapers lay in crumpled balls, kicked aside to make space for an incongruously neat table. Cutlery, glasses, napkins and mats surrounded two bottles, one of mine and one of theirs. I date feeling grown-up from the day I first bought wine for my parents. There was home-made soup, followed by four 'Lean Cuisines', followed by chocolate cake. 'Lean Cuisine', my mother assured me, was not a hint, it was just healthy and quick. She made first-class soups, said my father, and he made exceedingly good cakes, said my mother. One day they would open a restaurant and I would do the main courses.

That was how the conversation went, down familiar comfortable channels. I found myself relaxing, accepting that there was no hidden meaning in things that I had heard so many times before. The rituals were asserting themselves.

'I got nine out of ten in a spelling test,' said Sam, picking up a bone and smearing sauce over his face.

'So what's wrong with ten?' I said.

'No one gets ten.' His eyes over the bone were wide and peeved. 'Only Martin Jones who gets ten in everything, and Davey, who doesn't count.'

'Why doesn't poor Davey count?' Dad asked the inevitable question.

'He was just lucky, he doesn't work all the time.'

'Do you work all the time?' Me again, like an uncle to an unfamiliar nephew.

21

'No he doesn't,' said my mother. 'He watches too much television.'

Sam put down the bone and ran an exasperated hand through his short, spiky hair, like a tolerant man whose patience is being tried.

'And now you've got grease in your hair,' said my mother, running her fingers over his scalp and wiping some meat off his cheek. I wanted to reach out and touch his cheek too, and run my hand through his hair, but I was scared of offending him. I didn't know how to talk to him, or how to avoid impinging on his dignity.

He was looking at me. 'What do *you* do all day?'

I thought about it. 'Sometimes I watch a lot of tv too. I walk, I read, and think about things. Sometimes I go to town and wander, and I go to art galleries like a tourist. I see friends, sometimes, not recently . . .' Then this was how I spent my days. Was there nothing I had forgotten?

'Why can't you come away with us?'

'I can't afford it Sam, I'd like to.'

'Steve lives next to a lake, there'll be swimming and picnics. You could come, mum will pay.'

We laughed. I don't know why, but we all laughed.

'You could get a job then,' he said. 'On the bus on the way to school there are adverts for bus-drivers. You could drive my bus to school, then I wouldn't have to pay and you could pick me up outside the front door.'

'How are you for jobs?' asked my father, as if he had a couple in his wallet if I needed them.

'I've had another phase of writing letters,' I said. I had written two seven weeks earlier, on the first Monday after Helen left. 'People are on the look-out now.'

'Too choosy is your problem,' he said. 'Get on the ladder, and things will look different.'

My mother joined in. 'Because you can't afford that flat much longer, you know.'

'I manage.'

'How do you manage?'

'With dole and savings I manage.' For two years since leaving college I had had a succession of temporary jobs. Delaying tactics, my mother called them. How's your new delaying tactic going? she would ask. 'Trust me,' I said. 'You must trust me if you're going to abandon me all summer.' This time I was the only one who laughed. I wasn't engaged by the question of my future. My mind was on spelling-tests, and the uncomplicated perceptions of a seven-year-old. Perhaps that is the secret, I thought. Uncomplicated perceptions of the world.

After lunch I helped my father to complete a wall. I would have liked the room to stay just as it was, with the news getting older and older and the painting never quite finished, but I enjoyed working with him. Nothing needed to be said, and there was a casual satisfaction in making our efforts meet up in one bland colour in the middle.

In his new manner, my father reminded me of Molly, my mother's aunt. I thought of her in the silence as we painted. After her husband's death she had been liberated, my mother said. We visited her every year when I was a child, every winter, and for me she would turn the stories of her travels into exciting narratives. Her stories were about the Nile, Indian and American wildernesses, they were ingenious concoctions of fact and fiction. I was enchanted and, undismayed by her death, I used to long for old age to liberate me, to reveal to me a world of unimaginable freedom.

By the time we joined my mother in the garden I was tired, and glad to lie down. There is enough grass to lie there in unfiltered sunlight. There are low fences and gaps in the tumbly foliage which put my parents on intimate terms with their neighbours. It is a small, sociable garden.

The clouds came and went. We talked about the heat in Malawi, the cholera, and the darkness coming down like a blind each night. The plants would suffer no autumn and no spring, they would live an uninterrupted life.

There was a pause in the conversation, which stretched smoothly into a sleepy silence as the sun began to establish itself. The afternoon was lengthening effortlessly, like Sam's chewing gum. I raised myself on to my elbows to take a second look at my parents. They were looking older. My mother in fact was pale, so that her dyed black hair was too black. Her slim body and her small bare breasts made her fragile. My father was more robust, but much greyer than I remembered him, and the skin of his face was slack. It penetrated my ego, for a minute, that both of them looked mortal. More mortal than before.

Soon my father began to snore. A short irritable snort, a slowly expelled breath, a long, depthless silence. Snort, breath, silence . . . In the quiet garden it was as if someone had turned the volume up on life, and this was all there was to hear.

My mother turned to me with a frown of concentration.

'And how are you?'

'I'm fine.'

'Yes, but how are you?'

'Really, I'm fine. Up and down, you know.'

'More up than down?'

'Up *and* down. Both.'

'Have you talked to her at all? Or are you going to? I'm not trying, I mean I'm just saying, I think you should try talking.'

'Has she talked to me? She's gone, she's disappeared, I don't even know where she is.'

'Would it be difficult to find out? Of course not.'

'I don't know what I'm going to do.'

'I know. But I'm not asking for you to say that, I just want to suggest that you don't rule out, you know. Talking to her.'

'Well I'm sure I will.'

'But it's worth making the effort.'

'Could we please just change the subject please?'

'But I want to be able to help you.'

'I don't even know where she is.'

'Why won't you talk to me? We never really talk at all.'

Helen was instantly there too. 'You never really talk to your parents do you? I've noticed that. Why does Steve call you 'tight-lipped'? Why won't you give a little away? It worries me about you.' Her brown eyes were wide and angry, her lips were slightly apart, as if she was preparing to answer me before I spoke.

'I know,' I said, 'I know, I know.'

That was the moment that Sam came out of the house. He was

wearing pale blue swimming-trunks, and his thin white arms were swinging bravely. It was a beautifully timed arrival.

'You better get a tan,' my mother told him, in a strained voice, 'or you'll burn up in Malawi.'

'I know,' he said. 'He looked at me. 'Why is there a suitcase in the hall? Is it yours?'

'Yes,' I said. I turned to my mother as Sam ran up and knelt on the towel behind me. 'I was thinking before I might move in for a while. There's a ghost in my flat.'

'I don't understand,' she said.

Of course not. I looked up at the sky.

'And don't for God's sake take that as a vindication,' she said with a vehemence that surprised me. 'Don't show me that nobody-understands-me expression. No one's forcing you to feel left out, it's your *choice*. Please stop it.'

It was a day for mum to surprise me. We are a family that avoids confrontations. We deal in dishonesty and partial communication. But the familiar rituals were outmoded after all. It was like a science-fiction film in which a complete stranger inhabits the body of someone you know.

'I'm sorry, mum. I'll stop it shall I? I'll try and stop it.'

I pulled off my t-shirt so that I was half naked too, and we lay quietly for a while, until a persevering cloud found its way in front of the sun.

I turned over to find Sam still kneeling there, looking puzzled. I jumped up, ruffled his hair, picked him up by his arms and swung him round, leaning back and shuffling my feet quickly so that he was horizontal and really flying. When I put him down he staggered back drunkenly and laughed, putting his arms out to steady himself like a tightrope walker. He sat down heavily. 'Now I'm all *dizzy*.'

He looked up at me when things had stopped revolving around him. 'Is there really a ghost in your house?'

'Yes,' I said, 'there really is.'

My father groaned, waking up. 'What?' he said. 'What shall I say?' My mother leant over and stroked his forehead. 'Time to go in,' she said gently.

★   ★   ★

'You can still stay.'

We were in the hall, and I had just picked up my suitcase. 'I might as well be in the flat. The post will be coming there. I can come here if the money does get tight.'

'We've got a surprise for you,' said my father.

'Another?'

'We thought you might like the car.'

'For a while,' said my mother.

'We've insured it in your name while we're gone.' He gave me the keys. 'Take care of it now.'

I was tempted to smile at the sight of their grave faces. What were they handing over? The keys should have been older and heavier, too big to be pocketed so easily.

There was some leave-taking confusion as I hugged my mother before I got into the car, and half-embraced my father through the driver's window. My mother's arms spread around me tentatively. My father's eyes were wistful. Sam insisted on shaking hands.

'Don't forget to write,' said my mother. 'We'll write.'

'Bless you,' said my father, as if he was launching me, and I backed out of the drive and accelerated away, past the deserted school, and the pond and the church, feeling as if I was stealing the car for a second time.

At least on the first occasion I had enjoyed an initial sense of escape. My father was having a spiritual crisis while my mother was having a marital one, and neither of them was talking much. One day, unlicensed, I stole the car and drove to the coast, hoping to find an old friend who lived in Brighton. Instead I became lost, and ended up on an anonymous pebbly beach beneath a massive grey sky, staring at the sea and rehearsing what I would say when I returned. Gulls squealed their contempt and uttered high pitched screams. I loitered for a while in an empty amusement arcade, where even the machines were sleeping. A man appeared from a back door and grudgingly switched one on for me. It chattered excitedly, outwitted me easily, and congratulated itself with a series of burps and minor explosions as I left.

I begged for petrol, and left my birthday watch as surety with my address. And when I found my way home the next day the car had somehow acquired a vicious scrape along the side. Even now an interrupted, blotchy line remained visible.

So I was absconding again. Summer, the time of year for independence, and repetition. The rear-view mirror had been knocked out of place, and I caught my eye as I glanced into it. I was smiling. They shouldn't trust me, I'm not myself. I don't want to leave another stubborn scar but I can see it coming, because sometimes I can tell the future.

CHINESE WALLS

I adjusted the light by the bed, admired the expensive sketchpad on my knees, fingered its smart black cover, opened it at its first page and asked the consumer, without premeditation, in bold black ink:

'How would *you* advertise *Dash*?'

Then I told her how to go about it, pointing out that she didn't have to worry about cheap jokes and flashy pictures, because the results (in big capitals) spoke for themselves. Above the blurb and beneath the vital question my pencils drew a colourful, but serious, box of soap-powder.

'You see? There are things to do which prove that I can act.' As they had before, my words dropped loudly into the room, splashing the silence against the walls. That knack of being alone was still eluding me, I was still talking to Helen, in her absence. Silence is not a problem, I insisted, silence is a space to move in. But I no longer believed myself. Echoing my positive thoughts were negative ones: I *am* unable to act. Silence *is* a problem.

On Monday morning an advertising agency had been in touch. Thank you for your letter, we are interviewing next week. Is Monday all right for you? Mr Belgrave will see you at ten o'clock on Monday, with your portfolio. Mr Belgrave is our Creative Director. There was a reservoir of authority in the secretary's laid-back voice. Yes, I said, yes, yes . . . thank you.

Three unremarkable days had floated by, the fourth had almost gone now too, and suddenly it was a week since my parents had left, it was late June, and still nothing had been done. 'What do you do all day?' Sam had asked. What are you doing Sam? It's got to be better than this. Sometimes I just stay in bed. A clock radio wakes me up in the mornings with a pop song, and at night I find the same song still playing in my head, reducing the intervening day to a dream, or a fantasy experienced in turning from my left side on to my right. It seems that I go only to the bathroom and to the fridge, but the flat becomes increasingly untidy. It is my untidiness, not Helen's. I miss her clothes lying in piles on the floor, occupying some of the drawers and the wardrobe space. I miss her make-up in the bathroom and by the mirror in the bedroom, I miss her reflection, her smell, her smile and her irritating habits. I become increasingly scared. I feel I have nothing to do with my own life.

Thursday evening then, and one advert completed. With my fat pencil poised over the thick, chalky paper, I looked for inspiration from posters on the wall and rows of spines on the shelves. The room itself began to preoccupy me. Its character had changed since Helen left, now it was the sum of its parts, no more: four walls, mundane furnishings, belongings. Characterless, indistinguishable from the rooms and houses all around me, all over London, with their walls and furnishings and belongings. I felt a longing to distinguish myself from all the people I was suddenly aware of.

'Dear Steve,' I wrote, then scrubbed it out angrily.

No, that won't do. That won't do unless it's an advert for the Post Office.

I tore off the page, crushed it into a ball and threw it into a corner. This is a game, I told myself, in which I have something to do with other people's lives. That makes it a way to distinguish myself. It is a question of finding the right combination of words and pictures, information and propaganda, with which to sway people, influence their opinions, and nudge them towards a course of action. It is a game, and it is a bastardized form of control. On the next page, at the top, I drew a large stamp. A clumsy profile of the Queen stared impassively at the edge of the paper. Halfway down the page I drew a second stamp, this time giving it a postmark in grainy black letters: 'The Post Office Is Your Friend.' In the third picture the Queen had turned, revealing a daringly low décolletage, and she was winking at the consumer. She looked out at me, crudely drawn, her wink looking like a black eye. I couldn't make the leap of imagination, I couldn't imagine myself exercising any kind of control.

I turned the page. How many to go? Ten more? I started again.

Dear Steve,

How are you? How are your family? Only tell me if they're well, don't tell me the nephew I've never met is ill. Did I tell you I like Alice? Yes, I like Alice. I like her forthrightness. What's it like living with someone who's forthright? As you know, I know nothing about forthrightness. I don't care what mum tells you, do *not* ask me about Helen if you write back. I mean it.

I read the first paragraph. That distinguishes me, I thought, that sets me in a family context. I continued carefully, my eyes watching my moving hand.

I want to know how you get on with mum and dad. Are they turning into grandparents before your very eyes? It must be magic, the way someone looks at you, shows you his sleeves, turns around, turns back, and all of a sudden he's someone else. I include you – I don't even know who I'm writing to. Write back and tell me who you are. Shall I tell you how I imagine you? I like to imagine you on a verandah looking out over your lake, with a desert behind you and mountains bulging out of the sand to one side. The sun is bleeding over the horizon and a small boat is moving imperceptibly over the water. Is it approaching or moving away? Impossible to say. Insects buzz and chirrup as you and Alice sip long cool drinks and Daniel dreams contentedly in his cot.

No? Nothing like that at all? I didn't really think so, but it's nice to imagine. What is it like? Do they appreciate your Italian Air Force jacket? And your haircut? Do they actually cut hair in Malawi? I'm sorry, my jealousy is showing. The sun sets for me behind a boring row of houses. There's an invigorating park across the road, but I can't even see it, and at the moment I can't be bothered to cross the road anyway. I hate the city, I always have hated it. There are so many buildings there's no room for people. I have this fantasy, have I told you before? I imagine sometimes that the houses all disappear, and when I wake up and get to my feet there are eight million people around me stretching and yawning and looking around. No one wants to look foolish, so everyone pretends that they aren't surprised. We nod to our naked neighbours, and chat as we casually pull on some clothes. We wander a little way, and are instantly lost. Is this where my flat was, or was it on that hill? Is this where London was, or was it further up river? Only, on my present form, I wouldn't get up. Eight million people would look at me and think – what a lazy bastard. I don't know, I just don't see much point in moving just now. I mean any sort of moving. There's nowhere I want to go.

I'll tell you how I remember you. When I'm pissed off with you, or jealous, I think of this. You stopped going to Molly's soon after I started, but two or three times we all drove up together. We'd sit in the back, and mum and dad in the front, and we'd glide slowly up the motorway with plenty of stops for me to throw up in service-station car-parks. I was sick every time and I'd be miserable, but that's part of the beauty of it – all three of you were there, you were like three great filters between me and the world. I could *afford* to be helpless, or miserable. I could curl up on the back seat – mum was always saying 'Just go to sleep, you'll feel better' – and nothing else had to exist except the car and where we were going. I could close my eyes in London and open them four hundred miles away. Now I write it down it changes, I always thought it was a memory of you, not of me. I don't suppose it even really happened.

So much for control, I thought. Even speaking to my brother I don't know how much is true, how much is pose or pretension. I looked at the thick, untidy lines of the letters. He would have trouble deciphering some of it. What has happened to my ability to communicate? Brother, mother or lover, there seems to be a gulf that I can't bridge. It is like a failure of eyesight: everyone I look at is distorted, or out of focus, only dimly perceived. Try again. Watch yourself.

I understand being lonely Steve, but I don't understand why I'm scared. I feel I'm on the edge of something, or something is going to happen. I'm beginning to hate this letter, I hate writing things I can't say, but I'm a verbal coward, as you know. Look at this forest of 'I's. I'm lost in it. This one isn't going to be sent, it makes *me* cringe. I'm sorry. I wish I was with you, really, I wish I was with you now.

I wrote 'Love Simon' and then tore off the page and screwed it up. I held the letter in my fist and squeezed, as if the paper was responsible for what was written on it. It joined the first one in the corner.

On the next page I drew a girl at a writing desk, hand on forehead, staring at the wall. Underneath I wrote, 'Words may fail you, but the Post Office won't.'

I got out of bed and dribbled the letter around the room a little, and then sat on the edge of the mattress with it under my foot. I picked it up, uncrumpling it carefully as if untying a knot, finding the corners and lifting them outwards, unfolding the folds and smoothing the ridges over my thigh. It had become parchment, veined with creases, less legible than ever. I reread it, and then scribbled over the last paragraph and wrote, 'P.S. I have an interview on Monday,' underneath it. I folded it twice and stuffed it into an undersized envelope thinking – better this communication than none at all. Then, riding a sudden impulse, I phoned Helen's parents. What would I say? The phone rang, and continued to ring. Nothing. I thought of another possibility: before she moved in with me Helen shared a flat with a girlfriend in Clapham – perhaps she had returned there. Still not knowing what I planned to say, I dialled the number. A familiar male voice answered.

'Vince? Is that Vince? What are you doing there?'

That noncommittal tone of voice which precedes recognition: 'Living here. Who's this then?'

'It's Simon, hello Vince. I didn't know you'd moved in there, when did that happen?'

'Simon? No it's not, it can't be. Simon's in a monastery, he's a Trappist or something. No one's seen or heard from him.' A mock note of accusation: 'You've had the phone off the hook haven't you?'

'Only in the bath,' I lied. 'Well how are you? I was trying to get in touch with Helen really.'

'Listen I'm sorry about that,' he said, 'I mean I'm really sorry. I heard it was all finished. How are you coping?'

'I don't know how, I'm not thinking about it, that seems to work. You've seen her then?'

'We had a drink, she's been pretty miserable. It makes no sense, does it, when you're both miserable. You two should talk, you know. When can *we* have a drink meanwhile? Can you come out tonight? How are you anyway? You haven't told me yet. Tomorrow night maybe, it's a bit late isn't it, but phones are no good, we should meet, what you need I bet is a few drinks.'

I moved the receiver away from my ear. I felt bulldozed by this slightly false wave of sociability. There was an awkwardness involved in it, something covered up. No, was his answer, I can't come out just now, I'm not up to it, I haven't got the words. 'I'm really busy,' I said, and I told him about the interview and the portfolio.

'You've been keeping plenty to yourself,' he said, 'as usual.'

A note of irritation in his voice now? 'You know me, I'm not one for saying much.'

Silence, except for the crackling on the line. 'That much is true,' he said finally, flatly. 'No one I know would argue with that.' Was that a snide reference to Helen? 'Just don't go back in quarantine all right? All right?'

I made a sound which he took to be acquiescence.

'Get in touch after the interview, we really should talk, phones are no good, we should talk.'

I promised to call him on Monday night, and then we said goodbye and I put the phone down. I was sitting in the hall, on the floor in a dressing-gown, my fingers tapping the receiver as if I was waiting for a call. Brother, mother, lover, friend. My fingernails clicked on the plastic. A gulf, I was thinking, suggests something natural. It is not a question of gulfs separating people from people, it is a question of walls, man-made walls obscuring vision. I remembered Steve calling me tight-lipped, my mother thinking I harboured secrets, and now Vince resenting my reserve and telling me to talk to Helen: each of them made me angry. As if they had any right to preach. When so much is hidden in any case, what is the harm in opting out of verbal games?

Later, when I couldn't sleep, I sat up and wrote a slogan to attract bus-drivers: 'Don't ride it, drive it!'

I lay back and considered the positive resonance of the words, trying to take them to heart, repeating them like a prayer. If I could regain control over my life . . . The idea remained incomplete, my thoughts were not engaged. I gave up, and played patience.

On the night before the interview, I was belatedly cooking myself a meal, and trying to nurture a sense of achievement: almost the end of June, and activity at last. As I opened the oven door a gust of air made me recoil. I prodded the potato cautiously. Still not ready. I stabbed it with a knife, wincing at the heat, and shut the door.

Like a single, clearly shaped drop of water from a tap, a memory, self-contained, dropped into my mind. My perceptions seemed suddenly to sharpen. My father pulls me back as I poke semi-daringly at the hot charcoal. A few rockets scrape up into the sky, and a fat candle fizzes and flares in traffic-light colours. The bonfire waits. In the dark it is like a huge, clumsily erected tent, three or four times taller than me. Flames begin to nibble, then bite, then devour it, reaching up towards the hunched figure sitting awkwardly at the top. Karen and I drink something hot and very sweet. The sickly smell of the drink mingles with the smells of smoke, of bodies, of trampled grass and the almost exotic scent of burnt-out fire-works. Experimentally, I put an arm around her, one eye on the flickering faces of my friends dancing with sparklers nearby. In the embers of the barbecue the skewered, foil-wrapped potatoes are not quite ready.

For *our* games we steal off into the darkness on the edge of the party. Karen is sexless in her jeans and furry anorak. Our heads move, and our noses bump. Her lips are warm and hard. They are just lips.

She pulls away. 'I've got some fags,' she says.

They are a better game. Stolen from her mother, they are a more obvious transgression. She unzips a pocket and takes them out, creased and crooked. One leaks tobacco from a tear. We light them eagerly and with difficulty and find, as with the kiss, that their attraction is obscure. With their red tips we describe neat circles in the air, but we choke helplessly when we try to blow smoke rings. We hold them to one side as we kiss again, and my tongue pokes daringly between her lips. Our chokes become giggles as we run back to find some sparklers, before they run out.

What chain of events led me from there to a juvenile murderous fantasy, and to this isolation?

Still stranded in the past, I reached into the oven and picked up the knife in my bare right hand. In retrospect the pain and the awareness of what I have done come at the same time. 'Shit.' The word hardly left my lips in the quiet kitchen, hung on them while I stood still for another second, as if frozen rather than burnt.

Suddenly, motion. I threw the impaled potato into the sink, twisted the tap on and held my hand under the gushing water. I poked the skin and watched it change colour as the handle-shaped blisters swelled, thickened and creased as they were pushed backwards and forwards under my curious finger. Serves me right. Shit. I filled the sink and immersed my hand. The hairs swayed gently. What is wrong with me? The back of my hand looked white and lifeless but underneath, in my palm, my pulse throbbed and my skin continued to burn, as if to warn me that they were stubborn blisters and, like the stubborn scar on the car, they would remind me of transgression.

Ten men in glossy business suits seated around a sickle-shaped table. Toothy grins and grimaces. We were in a high place, and my position was precarious. Persistent, fruitless interrogation, centring on the question: 'Why?' Why did you do this? think that? wear that expression? give that response? fail to give this response? How should I know? I don't know, I don't understand, how can I know unless you explain? It was an unresolved dream, and when I slid back into my body as I woke up the relief was a physical electric sensation over my skin.

A song blared out of the radio just after I had drifted back to sleep. I turned it off and dozed uneasily, aware now of the pain in my hand. I touched my palm to the sheet, to the wall and to the window, trying to cool it and soothe it. Things were too warm.

The light in the bathroom hurt my eyes. I shaved and cut myself. Bristles scattered in the sink like chocolate chips on the ice-cream enamel. I held some toilet paper to my chin while I studied myself. Thin face. Bags under the nervous eyes. Untidy hair retreating from the forehead. Untidy banadge on the hand. 'Use *Dapper* after-shave,' my reflection mocked me, 'because women love a *Dapper* man.'

I wasn't tempted to take the car. At least get there safely, I told myself. The station was busy, and I joined a long queue climbing the stairs to the ticket-office. It crept forward like a lazy sinuous animal. I was herded into my seat on the tube and held there immovably. I studied the patterns of dirt on the window, felt the rough texture of the seat, and read the thoughts of the man sitting opposite.

'You don't feel involved, but you know damn well that you are.' His eyes moved around slyly, including the whole carriage, while his head remained bent over the newspaper. 'You know damn well that you are involved. It's lucky someone can see through you because you'll never see through yourselves. You should be glad you've got me, I'm your interpreter.' A smile escaped at this, as far as the corner of his mouth. 'You're all Chinese, hiding behind your Chinese walls, and I'm your interpreter.'

No reaction. People stared at the floor or the roof and avoided each other's eyes.

The man put the paper down and rested his head against the seat. A grey-haired type with an almost monkish bald spot. Fairly smartly turned out except for a superfluous beige anorak over his suit. Grudge-bearing eyes which examined his fellow passengers with the care of a conscientious doctor. He was toying with the idea he had found: 'You're all Chinese, that's the underlying problem. You can't understand yourselves, I can't understand you – what do you expect?' The eyes darted from side to side, as if what he expected was contradiction. 'A different culture, worlds apart. A different language. What do you expect from the race which built the longest, widest, tallest wall imaginable?'

He was leaning against the window now, grim-faced. Monday-morning weariness. We had emerged from a tunnel and he was examining the view with those same grudge-bearing eyes. Flats and factories, factories and flats, a great heap of wrecked cars, a tall chimney. Arid landscape. 'Something is catching up with us, and soon it will overtake us.' His thoughts, prompted by his view, spiralled downwards. 'It lives here: repulsion between individuals instead of attraction, bouncing apart instead of cohesion. One day we'll all wake up, all of us, and we'll have yellow skin and we won't recognize our houses and we'll be talking a language we can't understand. We won't understand what other people are saying, and we won't even understand what we say ourselves.'

The train stopped, waiting for a platform to clear ahead, and the man's eyes focused. A smile appeared, and reached both corners of his mouth. High above us a man in blue overalls was standing on a roof holding a saucepan, feeding the birds. A pigeon was perching on the edge of the saucepan, pecking at its contents, and as we watched another was coming, wheeling around his shoulders. As far as we could tell from so far below him, the man didn't flinch as it landed on his wrist, and then hopped up to join the first. What I felt, watching him, was a sense of relief: petty kindnesses still exist, and so do avenues of escape. Up there he was jostled only by the birds and the breeze, the buildings were all below him, like so many hills of dirt. He stood, not at the top of the town, but at the foot of the sky, and the whole wide world was around him. If he stretched out his arms, I thought, he might fly.

As the man opposite me looked back into the carriage our eyes met and, making absurd my interpretation of his demeanour, he smiled pleasantly.

My thoughts, directed by the bird man, took a new turn. I remembered my aunt again, I remembered her kitchen, and the smell of it, pastry, and leaving it, crunching snow underfoot, to feed birds in her garden with torn-up pieces of sliced white bread. The picture in my mind was of a snow-covered lawn and a great flock of birds descending around me like a cloud. On a moonlit night the snow would seem to shimmer with a light of its own, and the darkness would hang suspended above it. So much simpler to dwell on these vivid images and memories. My aunt's stories continued to dictate my dreams, long after she died. So much simpler to preserve the puzzled perspective of a child.

A case knocked my shin, and the door opened. We had arrived at the station while I stood on my aunt's lawn.

I picked up my sketchpad and walked slowly down the long platform. Brushed aside by other, faster-moving commuters, held up by a cross-current moving from another platform, squeezed up the escalator like liquid through a narrow nozzle, I finally joined the tail-end of the crowd at the ticket-barrier. I felt like tapping people on the shoulder and asking who they were. Are you sure you're in the right place? It's just that I don't recognize you. I mean, are you sure you're supposed to be here? Perhaps it's me but, something is not quite . . . not altogether right. For instance, where exactly have you all come from? Is there something you want to tell me?

The crowd filtered through the barrier.

I won't mind, if you'll just tell me I promise I won't mind.

Outside, the street flowed like a river. I had to keep moving to stay upright. Unused to such crowds, I found myself stepping on heels, and being stepped on in return, and collided with and cursed. Going more or less at the speed of the current I was right on time when I reached the building, but I didn't go in, I edged out of the flow and stood opposite, staring upwards. It was a bright tower, like a bulky, angular chimney, reaching far higher than the bird man had stood. Towards the top a window-cleaner's cradle clung to the side. A man was washing the reflection of a cloud.

I walked on until I saw a small, not too crowded café, and I slipped in, feeling like someone sheltering from bad weather. A lady in a long white apron gave me a generous smile. 'Bit tired dear? What can I get you? Just sit down for a while my love, and rest your feet.' I felt like telling her my life-story, and receiving some wise advice in return. She would hint, unconsciously, at some surprising but suddenly inevitable course of action, and I would recognise my cue. Things would fall into place. The world is full of clues, if only I can piece them together.

I slouched into a seat far away from the window. I leant against the wall, ignoring my coffee, thinking I could still be asleep, thinking I *was* more or less still asleep. The glossy red seats were crammed together, but it was not claustrophobic. There was an almost studious air in the shady stillness. The urn at the counter steamed industriously. Cups were raised with slow care, heads bent slowly, eyes rested on newspapers.

The mandarin who was waiting to interview me was at the top of the building, seated behind a wide, richly varnished desk in a huge leather swivel chair. He was hidden in it, looking through his wall-window at the city lying beneath him. The office was papered with posters advertising various products. In one corner a stack of video recorders brooded next to a pile of televisions. Opposite them a small stool crouched in front of a vast drawing board beside a leafy green stem, writhing as if in pain. Shelves contained an organised litter of executive toys, knickknacks, curios and books, big volumes like slabs of colourful paving. Supermarket music murmured from an indefinite number of invisible speakers.

He swings around. A small man, a fat face over an expensive suit and a shiny tie. Eyes lost in wrinkles. He raises his arms to me, and there is a glint of cufflinks and clean fingernails. As my face changes in recognition he smiles outrageously, so broadly that it hides his features, a mutant teeth-revealing smile that slashes his face. He waves a hand at the city and it shrinks back from him nervously. The city is his creature. On the desk now is a swordstick. Still smiling, he reveals a shining inch of the blade. Finally, he speaks.

'Welcome back young man,' he says. 'I believe we have an account to settle?'

I left the café, forded the pavement, stepped through an unmoving line of traffic, came out of it looking the wrong way and was snatched up and flung down again by the corner of a blue Volvo screeching, a little too late, to a stop. The impact was like a mallet swung by a lumberjack against my knee, sending me pirouetting, but it was all right, it wasn't too serious, because the surface of the road was cushion soft, and the left leg, the leg that was hit, didn't hurt at all. I couldn't feel it at all. Fairly soon there was no noise either, just that screech that ended very quickly and then echoed on and on, quieter and quieter, like ripples on a pond.

The man at the left-hand end of the sickle shaped table leant forward and clasped his hands in front of him.

'We have a new product.'

I tried to find an appropriate answer, but I had nothing to say.

The next man leant forward. 'We're very excited about it.'

Still no response.

'It should appeal to everybody.'

'It's a question of image enhancement.'

A prompting from the fifth man: 'What are your thoughts?'

One by one around the table they leant forward, clasping their hands, making their contributions, trying to nudge me into speech, betraying increasing impatience. 'We'd value your input.' 'We feel there's no place for taboo in our society.' 'Tell us your thoughts, we do want to know.' 'Tell us your thoughts.'

I looked from one to another like an actor who has forgotten his lines. 'I don't know,' I said. 'What is the product? Can you explain the context? I'd like to help you, I'm not sure you understand . . .'

But, as I knew they would, they mistook my confusion for indifference, or arrogance, and they seemed ready to spit at me. They turned to each other now, as if I had already left, and continued to discuss the subject, just as if I had left and my seat was empty. Speechless, I could only watch, shifting uncomfortably.

Finally the first one leant back again in his chair, rested his head on his hands, and interrupted the others.

'Is he awake?'

'Matter of time.'

'Lucky to be alive.'

I tried to move then but I couldn't, beyond scraping my fingers on the road surface. The pain in my knee was suddenly excruciating, and a spasm went through my body. 'Don't try to move,' came the response, someone leaning over me, telling me not to worry, not to try to move, everything was o.k. Perhaps my eyesight was blurring, but wasn't there a crowd around me? Everyone looking at me, why was I suddenly the centre of attention? Was there something I should say to all these people, some formula of conventional words I had forgotten? Still speechless. Another question: who should they call for me? An image of all these people on the telephone together, a symphony of voices. Groping for an answer I thought of my mother and my family but they were too distant, too far away, and I said I wanted to see my aunt again, I'd like to see my aunt please and could they please arrange it for me?

JULY

BECALMED

While I slept, June ended and July began.

I discovered stillness.

I lay in the Emporium like one of its artefacts, waiting for a buyer. The defunct ward was back in use, bleached in white light now, draining the colour from everything. People spoke to me but I didn't understand them. Mr Pock visited once, and his small hands squeezed and probed at my left knee, pinching the swollen, inflated flesh. He chuckled, and winked at me amiably, and before he left he pressed a red-hot coin into my right hand.

I lost a day or two, and when I woke I was as white as a sheet. It was the nurse's fault. Her uniform was a whisper of blue. She bent over me to adjust a pillow and I smelt the starch of her apron: it brushed my cheek and I was infected, bleeding to white. I raised my hand, and it was so pale that I could watch a tinge of pink pulsing sluggishly beneath the skin.

'Don't move yet my love.'

But, when I was fully awake, stillness abandoned me. It was doctor's orders. She toured the ward with her students like a swan with her cygnets, and they clustered around my bed almost accidentally, as if it was in the way. There was some cursory mention of concussion and contusions, my eyes were stared into, and the bump on my head was examined while I sat up with my chin on my chest as if praying. 'Have a rest,' said the doctor, 'and you can leave us tomorrow. The physio will come and see you this afternoon. Just bend your leg for us?' I bent my leg for them, until my heel was about a foot from my inner thigh. 'That's fine,' she said, 'well done. Come back and see us soon.'

They moved on to a more stimulating case, and I watched them. My surroundings gradually became more realistic. I watched nurses

45

glide back and forth. None of them spared me a glance now, and I began to feel as if the doctor had stamped 'Tested and Approved' on my forehead. Perhaps it was difficult to distinguish me from my sheets. They were stiff as cardboard, filling my nostrils with their disinfected smell. But I felt almost healthy later in the morning, when a body arrived on the ward, unconscious and wrapped in bandages, wheeled in by two porters. It was placed indelicately on a bed, tucked in by a nurse, and left with a cage inserted over its plastered leg. After an hour it began to sing. The words were a tuneless lament which, convinced by their own plangency, ended in harsh, dry sobs.

'Fuck you then,' croaked the body. 'Fuck you.'

When it woke up it moved its head around vaguely, like a small child. It was dosed with enough painkillers to send it drowsing back to sleep.

The afternoon had its highspot too, when the physiotherapist arrived.

'Mr Hare?'

'Simon.'

She smiled and sat on the edge of the bed, leaning a pair of crutches against the cabinet.

'Now then, show me a bit of leg.'

I pushed back the sheet, then gingerly moved my leg outwards. I pulled the sheet back into place and laid my leg on top of it.

'Do that again,' she said, 'but bend your leg towards you instead of moving it outwards.'

I reversed the procedure and then did as she said, as if I was operating a fragile mechanical device. My foot became entangled with the sheet, because I couldn't get it far enough up the bed.

She peeled up the bandage.

Underneath the final, transparent layer of dressing I saw that my knee was covered by an exotic growth. A livid purple egg-sized lump grew shiny black lettuce-leaves backwards, encircling my leg. They were at once taut and wrinkled, as if hiding wormy creatures beneath. My knee was no longer my own, it was a malevolent thing clinging to my leg. When I saw it, I wanted to shrink away from it.

Surely it had nothing to do with me. Couldn't they remove it? Wasn't that why I was here?

'Mmmm,' said the physiotherapist. 'That's a bit of a mess isn't it?'

She picked up the crutches. 'Swing your legs off the bed. No weight on it now.'

She taught me to hobble. I moved cautiously up and down between the lines of beds and received the criticism and encouragement of their occupants, like a costumed entrant in a beauty contest. I felt skin and pus jostling in my palm. A stinging dampness told me that another blister had burst.

When she left, the phsyio was satisfied that I could carry my leg without using it. She gave me a programme of exercises to do, and then said goodbye.

'Are you going home now?'

'It's five 'o'clock isn't it?'

'I might see you next time then.'

'Take care.'

My words could not really reach her, certainly could not retain her. I watched her leave, her blue-trimmed white coat turning a corner.

That night the creature shifted restlessly on my knee, snuggling up, always trying to wrap itself tighter, like a baby's fist around a finger. I raised my leg a few inches, keeping it straight and pulling my toes towards me. Raised and lowered . . . raised and lowered. I bent it towards me as far as it would comfortably go, and then, with a hand on my instep, I tried to pull it closer. I watched the movements of the night-nurse. She paid particular attention to the body, now revealed as the victim of a motorbike accident. She visited him every hour, taking his temperature, his blood pressure and his pulse, and checking the drip that fed him. I didn't sleep, I watched her visits, fascinated by her careful movements. The way she lifted his wrist, as if it was fragile, and might break in her hands.

Still vague, I had to stand by the door for a while, to let the intoxicating colour and the noise and the smell of the fresh air gradually return to me. Where to? I caught a few glances thrown my way, and read my identity in them: a pale-faced post-accident man. I gazed back resentfully. Privately, I drained their faces of colour, gave them crutches and slings and wide-eyed nervous stares, until the street was full of shambling casualties.

My parents' house received me like a stranger. The ambulance which dropped me on its rounds left me standing in the drive staring at the place like a hitch-hiker dumped in the middle of nowhere. I opened the door to an awkward silence. The sun on the newly painted walls was clinically bright, the clutter in the kitchen had been discreetly tidied, the cushions on the sofa were arranged in fussy symmetry. Only my own room welcomed me back: the same books were on the same shelves, the same scratches on the desk. This is the view. I was the missing article, making the picture complete, filling in a space to create a whole. This is the smell, and this is the touch of the sheets. The sheets are tender to me now.

I thought that a little time to myself might be just what I needed, gathering strength before trying to meet people. So, the next day I made an effort to organise my time. Stillness is clearly impossible but a little organisation, I thought, is a fair second best. If I limited sensations and experiences, then there need be nothing to be afraid of. A neighbour picked up a week's provisions for me at the supermarket. For the rest of the week I would stay around the house and convalesce. I plundered my parents' shelves and, after lunch, took a selection of books into the garden. The sun shone gamely, and when I opened a book it reflected too brightly off the page. I found myself skimming over the lines, turning the page before I had had time to read a paragraph. Soon the books lay like a pillow within my folded arms, or like ballast I was hugging to myself. In the peace of the afternoon, cries from the school half a mile away seemed to be addressed to me. I closed my eyes and left the books and the garden to enter the playground. Football was going on, and a game of tag was threading the players, getting in the way, occasionally appropriating the ball. Running, hurled insults, the senstation of exclusion. Underlying this, the sweaty itch beneath my bandage was buzzing like a muted bell, pulling me back to the garden. The buzzing played a counterpoint to the playground cries, and then began to swell above them, returning me to the garden, reminding me of warmth and the heaviness of my body, until, after scratching uselessly at my knee, I gave up and limped back into the house.

I found it impossible to stay there for long. Soon I took short repetitive walks, around the old landmarks, establishing that this was familiar territory, not the middle of nowhere. While the school watched from the edge of the village, the church was forever setting sail in the lake of grass. I returned every day, as if expecting to mark some progress in its journey. I would circle it, and stand staring up at it, and then turn around self-consciously, wondering what must I look like, hanging around here, day after day? I needn't have worried. Only my shadow ever watched me, hard-edged, four-legged, hunched at my heels patiently. Those I did see I stared at as if my eyes had the power to give them the crutches and the sick pallor that I imagined.

My habits became sluggish and, restless both in the house and out of it, I realised that I had been optimistic about my ability to organise my time. There was too much of it. I could not coerce events into manageable shape when I was so swamped by time. Days were baggy and elastic, it took forever to cross them from end to end. After a week of restricted movement and no activity I was nostalgic for the stale routine of the hospital. The question returned: where will I be at the end of the summer? July now, and still nothing happening. Organising, evaluating: I am no closer to knowing why Helen left me, no closer to decisions about my future. I dwell on the past, I walk forward looking over my shoulder. To be here is a regression. I have not called Vince, because he would be affable and evasive like my father. No one's forcing you to feel left out, my mother told me. Maybe, but the walls are still intact. Helen's silence in particular is effective.

The only decision I made in that time was a firm and vindictive one: I will make it my business, I thought, to break down Helen's walls.

When things began to happen, they took me by surprise. On the Monday of my second week at home I visited the launderette, loaded with bags like a Christmas shopper handicapped by gifts. They swung dangerously against my crutches, threatening my balance. In a grimy back room I gave the attendant a five-pound note and she doled out coins from a biscuit tin, her manner grudging and cautious, as if we were involved in an illicit exchange. Stuffed with clothes, my machine shuddered and shook as if they had come to life and were trying to get out. The orange plastic basket bulged and dripped as the woman carried it across the shop for me, hugging it to her long blue coat. I looked through a pile of ragged, coverless magazines while the drier droned steadily. Soothingly. I began to read a magazine but it was so boring that my eyelids grew heavy. Apparently the walk had exhausted me, a short walk in warm weather. Well, the bags hadn't helped. I should buy a rucksack, a rucksack would improve things . . .

I woke up to find that the machine still droned and the attendant was talking on the phone to someone, to her husband by the sound of it. She looked quite different as she talked to him, unaware of my eyes; she stood up straighter, and she was smiling as if he was standing opposite her. It came to me that what I had seen in her earlier was a reflection of my own manner: the sour mistrust of Mr Pock. I trembled, feeling that he had been there as I slept, whispering into my ear, seducing me with boredom and self-pity. I was stepping backwards, stepping back, regressing. Suddenly in a disorderly hurry, almost tripping over myself, I bundled my clothes out of the drier and left, shouldering open the door, barging through like a vandal.

I stumbled through the village quickly, as if I might physically leave my confusion behind. I found that I could swing my left leg ahead of me with the crutches, a dead weight, pulling me forward. I got as far as the grass at the edge of the heath before, inevitably, I fell, tangled in crutches and bags. Somehow I had done no damage. I had fallen not on my outstretched leg, but on my right side, scattering the clothes as if to soften the impact. I gathered them without standing up, and then took a breath, sitting on the grass at the side of the road. Opposite me a delivery van was waiting to be unloaded. I was looking straight at it as I sat there, and its shape gradually emerged from the background, and then became sharply defined in my gaze. Its sliding door was wide open, revealing layer after layer of flowers, like an audience, heads out facing me in multi-coloured bunches. The internal organs of the van, superbly coloured, laid bare in cross-section. Reds and greens, bright yellow, orange brighter still, vivid purple, a library of colours, sitting out on the hot road. Here was a clue, not to be ignored. A man came and pulled a bunch, and it grew instantly into an extravagant green spray. Standing now, weighed down by my bags of heavy, damp clothes, I watched him with the respect a child has for a conjuror.

That was when I began to plan my escape.

Walking slowly now, someone with no need to hurry, I measured my desires against my resources and settled on Paris, before I had even reached home. After the out-patients' appointment tomorrow, my last savings could buy a flight there. Travel in style. I knew a friend to stay with until I found work. I would learn the language. Grudge-bearing Mr Pock wouldn't follow me that far, I would shake him off at the airport, even now he was shying away in surprise.

That afternoon Vince rang.

I was sitting on the kitchen floor suffering a painful titillation from a teatowel full of ice draped on my knee. I crawled over to the phone, trailing the crushed ice like immaculate droppings.

'Simon you bastard, you were going to call me.'

And now that I had decided to leave, I felt ready to see him. I explained about the accident, fielded his concern, and asked when we could meet.

'No excuses,' he said, 'we'll meet tonight. The Jester at about seven. And guess what, Helen will be there too.'

He had to go, the boss had just walked in. I gathered the melting ice and put the teatowel back on my knee, ignoring the shrinking shiver of my skin. Very well, I was thinking, a parting chat. We meet the first embarrassment with a polite kiss, near the lips. She jokes about my leg: there must be easier ways not to get into advertising. She wants a dignified return to friendship. We are adults after all. We talk about the future.

But disrupting these thoughts were others, underpinning, undermining, any dignified adult responses. She is lying beneath a thin sheet, her eyes closed, the lashes like feathers. The in-curving slope of her throat glides down to her collarbone. Her breasts rise smoothly to the lip of the sheet. The cotton stirs as she breathes. I kiss her and she wakes. She loves me more than ever.

It is her face below mine, the smell of her and the touch of her skin. Her ponytail of hair hanging down, in my palm, in my face. There is a longing that insists on being recognised, because she left without a reason, as if there was no responsibility between us, as if I was nothing to her. She has left me no room for a rational response.

I arrived at The Jester at twenty past seven, tired out by my journey, my left leg hanging beneath me like a sack of sand. There was a crush of three-piece suits surrounding the bar and thinning out hardly at all up to the walls. Smoke, sweat and a steady babble of voices almost overwhelmed me. What was being said? I couldn't distinguish any words from the noise. I pushed and slid awkwardly this way and that, inhaling other people's alcohol-heavy conversation, shouldering drinks out of the way, elbowing stomachs, kicking ankles and grinding ferrules into feet.

'Excuse me . . . ex*cuse* me? Sorry . . . sorry . . .'

Mr Pock pulled me along by the wrist. Get out of the fucking way. Why did she choose this place? Because she wants to avoid a conversation?

Squeezing between two backs I caught sight of a table occupied by people that I knew. There was Vincent's blond hair and rosy complexion. No Helen. Then who were these other people? What was I supposed to have to do with them? A face I didn't recognise rose and fought its way to the bar, with me at its shoulder. I interrupted as he ordered a variety of beers.

'Are you with Vincent?'

'Yes . . .' Eyebrows raised.

'My name's Simon Hare.'

'Simon!' A hearty handshake, and I found that I winced as if the fortnight-old blisters were still fresh. 'I've heard about you,' he said. 'What have you done to yourself? Let me buy you a drink.'

I let him buy me a drink, and I followed in his wake back to the table. Space was made for me to sit next to Vincent.

'Fuck me,' he said, 'we meet at last. Are you all right? You're very pale.'

'Tired,' I said. 'I'm already tired. How are you? How's business?'

'Me? I'm fine, budding company director aren't I? You know me. Listen I'm sorry about your bust-up. I told you already, didn't I? I'm sorry. What are you up to now anyway?'

'Not much,' I said. 'Perhaps I'm a budding advertiser. I'm really thinking about a holiday. It's what I need.'

Someone started talking about his travels in China, and I subsided into silence. A piercing laugh from the table behind us punctuated his words and my thoughts, while an argument somewhere near the bar made him keep raising his voice. A budding advertiser? I was thinking, I am more likely to be a budding patient. Life would go on elsewhere, making no demands on me. The egotism of illness allows me to expect attention. Helen sits on the bed. When the nurses aren't looking she leans over to kiss me. My hand cups a breast. She laughs. 'Not *here!*'

I had almost to shout to be heard: 'You said Helen was coming tonight?'

'So she said, so she said.' What was in that tone, and in that smile? The eyes of the others at the table were on me. For the first time I realised that Vincent might have replaced me, and now I remembered his awkwardness when we had talked before the accident. Piecing together the clues. Things fell into place.

Someone asked me a question.

'Sorry, I wasn't listening.'

He repeated it but I still couldn't hear, or couldn't understand. His words had degenerated into sounds.

He was saying it one more time, I was watching his lips, when Vincent interrupted, 'Look at that,' and at the same time someone stumbled into our table. A small compact man, bulging out of shirtsleeves; I had an impression of a taut, round stomach, fat arms and a thick neck, before he was up and rushing at someone, if you can rush over two steps. His sweat-darkened shirt stretched over his back and shoulders. There wasn't much to see, the man he was fighting was taller, a look of complete surprise on his face – How

53

did this happen? – before both were cut off from our table by people closing around them. Shouts and scuffles and a lot of manoeuvring by people who wanted to be involved and people who didn't.

I took the opportunity, said something, smiled and shrugged and left the table.

Outside, the walls of the side-street seemed to converge above me. No fresh air here, and soon the fighters might be ejected behind me. The face on the pub's sign grinned down, winking hugely. I was trying to orient myself when Vincent came out and grabbed my arm, so that I almost lost balance.

'Are you all right?' he said. 'Shit, I bet that was the last thing you needed.'

'I'm fine, I think I just better go home. I'm very tired.'

'No, don't go.' He was still holding my arm eagerly. 'I know it's difficult, it's not exactly the ideal place anyway, but stay, stay, we should talk, we really should.'

I think he felt the wave of aggression run through me, I think that's why he dropped my arm. I was as surprised as he was, and I tried a smile. 'It's not on, Vince. I know I haven't talked to you for about a decade, but now isn't the time.'

'All right,' he said. 'O.k. I'll tell Helen you were here if she turns up. Can I give her a message or something?'

'I'd like to get in touch with her.'

'I don't know,' he said. 'I mean I don't know what her number is.'

'Never mind.'

He went back inside. Never mind. I reminded myself of my decision: I was leaving soon, and beginning again. Even my family would come back and wonder where I was. The door swung shut behind him, muffling the noise from within. Again, I felt a sudden, disarming longing for the peace of the hospital bed, and the unchallenging company of boredom.

I walked past St Paul's and on to the middle of Blackfriars Bridge, resting my crutches on the low stone wall there and leaning on it, testing my weight on my left leg. There was no more than an irritable stirring from the diminished creature on my knee.

Ownership was being returned to me. I stood on two legs, feeling I could have stayed there all night, releasing one long, deeply held breath.

A row of variously labelled bottles stands before a long mirror which reflects the scene in front of me. The tables are afloat among the seated bodies, each a still-life study ready to drift out of the bar in search of new patterns of light and shade. The air is sweet. I take a breath and join the conversation of the crowd of friends around me. From here we go on to a restaurant, where sometimes I meet a family I have come to know. Mid-July, there are still Parisians in Paris. The youngest son recognises me and runs over and jumps on to a chair so that, eye to eye, he can persuade me to join them. He would climb on to the table if I let him. Afterwards M. Marsaud insists that I return home with them for coffee and more drinks. He is a grey-haired old man, something of a gourmet, with an eccentric taste in suits. His wife is both aristocratically elegant and unreservedly affectionate. They recognise that a romance is growing between me and their eldest daughter, and they hope that it will blossom. They often remark how fluently I speak their language.

When I got home the phone was ringing. It was Helen, shouting over the noise of the pub, apologising for arriving so late. Was I all right? What had happened to my leg? Why had I left? Talking to her, this much-anticipated event, came to me easily. An air of detachment had settled on me since I left the pub like a heavy, muffling overcoat. I said that I couldn't talk now, that I was about to go to bed, but I would like to see her. We arranged a date. 'This Sunday then,' she said, 'definitely. I can't wait to see you.' Oh definitely, I thought, there's so much to be said. Still dreaming about my imminent escape to Paris, I began to consider what might be the best, if not the most tasteful way of organising my reunion with Helen.

The next morning I found that the hospital was a less personal place in the daylight of consciousness. I had thought that the clientele was quite exclusive, I hadn't realised that so many were held up or stalled here by ill health.

The foyer was as crowded as a department store at sale time. Customers jockeyed for position around the Appointments desk, as if eager for bargains. Nurses mingled like shop assistants. A lot of healthy-looking people were milling around, but it was impossible to tell if they were doctors, drivers, in-patients, out-patients or visitors. It seemed to me at the time that all of them were patients.

I joined the queue in the waiting room. The seats were arranged timidly around the walls, circling a table piled, as in the launderette, with aging magazines. My stiff leg and crutches lay in the path of the unwary nurses and patients who passed in both directions. Who would have believed there were so many?

'My grandmother was always having trouble with her boundaries.'

I turned. The lady on my right was talking to herself. One arm, cased in plaster, pressed a hand against her navel, as if she was scratching an insistent itch. Her free hand drew shapes in the air which at first she seemed to be addressing. Then she turned, and I realised that she was talking to me.

'People would come in the dead of night and move her fence posts. She didn't know *where* she was. She didn't know who they were.'

I didn't know where I was. If I had had a phrase book I might have known how to answer her. Beneath her mottled, blue-veined skin was an amber complexion. The crow's feet and folds around her eyes disguised their slant. I paid attention to her gestures, wondering if sign language might be the key.

'It wasn't a question of who to suspect. Naturally she suspected everybody. But what was she to do?' She met my eyes now, her lips pursed and her head slightly tilted. 'What was she to do?'

I was let off the hook by the man on my left. As he began to express sympathy I shrank back in my chair to allow the conversation to continue over my lap. I became conscious of my hands. A fist clenched and unclenched. I picked anxiously at a fingernail as the remarks, sometimes simultaneous, sometimes alternating, continued to be exchanged.

'Mr Hare?'

It was a relief to enter the doctor's office. At once I knew that rules began to apply. He was a tall man, with short dark hair and a moustache. He shook hands formally. Again I winced slightly, as if the blisters were still in full bloom. But what is that to me? I have nothing to do with omens. I have plans now, a plan to talk with Helen and a plan for my escape. Order has been imposed now, there are safe limits to move within.

I took off my shirt and lay down for an examination. It is a flattering process. A serious man is taking you seriously. You surrender responsibility to him, and he inspects your hands and fingernails, eyes and armpits, as if they are significant. My goodness, my body! You look at it yourself with a stranger's eye. Not so bad, not so bad I suppose. A few press-ups each night and it would be quite respectable.

He pushed and probed at my yellow-and-mauve-streaked knee. Another wince as he pressed a particular area. And how should I interpret this particular wince? That is the beauty of the situation – interpretation may safely be left to the doctor. He is a man with authority. He pressed again, with his fingertips, harder now, as if moulding a shape beneath the skin. Obediently, I bent the leg for him, lifted it and moved it from side to side.

'I see you've been doing your exercises, Mr Hare,' he said. 'Your muscles are in fine shape, considering. Have you put very much weight on it?'

I explained, with some complacency, that I had begun to walk with one crutch, and without assistance in the house.

'Very good,' he said, 'very good.' A tuft of hair nodded its agreement over his forehead. 'We'll give you a stick next, that should be sufficient. I think we'll have a couple of x-rays too. The nurse will tell you where to go, and if you'd like to wait, I can perhaps see the pictures.'

Of course, of course I'd like to wait. Just as you say. Let's round off this episode before I move on. A clean slate is what I'm after.

I was led to another row of seats, in the corridor outside the x-ray room. More waiting; once more, leg and crutches formed a minor barricade. I had to half stand to allow a trolley to be wheeled around me and into the room behind. I saw a small face beneath wisps of white hair. It was all eyes, spying this way and that as if all the body's motion was now invested in them, as if it was imperative not to miss anything.

I was next. I lay still as the big machine above me hummed. First on my back, and then on my side. My skin tickled as the x-rays peered beneath it. I stood pressed against a cold wooden board for a chest x-ray, shoulders back and holding my breath as if on parade. Formalities. I was prepared to conform to them, but I was becoming bored. The novelty had worn off with the tedious waiting and I was ready for the machinery to spit me out: Tested and Approved.

The nurse conveyed me back to the waiting room, and eventually back to the doctor's office. He was sitting at his desk, dark-suited now, his white coat hanging in the corner like a silent accomplice. Behind him, two ghostly x-rays were attached to an illuminated plate. Milky white bone lay on a cloudy bed of tissue. He began to speak as the nurse was leaving, before she had even closed the door.

'Our mistake,' he said, 'was not to take any lateral pictures when you were with us before.' He smiled, although his moustache continued to frown, as he stood up. 'But it was natural enough. We were looking for a fracture of the patella.'

'Yes,' I nodded. And then, 'What are you looking for now?'

'Have you had much pain in the knee?'

His shoulders remained still, but his head leaned forward, as if he didn't want to miss a nuance of my answer. I wondered if he wore his hair short at the sides to keep it free of his ears.

'It's been tender,' I said. 'And there's a sort of dull ache that doesn't go away. What are you saying exactly?'

He looked at his coat, as if he would have liked to consult with it, but felt constrained by my presence. 'Nothing really, just yet. Let me show you what's worrying us.'

Us? Him and the coat?

He turned at last to the x-rays waiting behind him. Like a teacher instructing a slow pupil, he pointed at a white smudge on the picture, behind the kneecap. His explanation was directed mostly at the smudge.

'This is the fellow. A fragment of bone, or perhaps a calcified haematoma' – he turned momentarily to smile – 'a blood clot. That's what it ought to be. Muscular wastage is minimal, your neuro-vascular pack is intact, your chest x-ray is clear. What I'm saying is don't worry. We'll book you in for a body scan and a C.T. in a couple of days, and we'll find out what it is. I'm afraid we may want to perform a biopsy.'

He turned now, and smiled at me again, as if we were discussing performing the school play.

'Well what do you think it *might* be?'

'You see there's not really any mileage in speculating. We'll see you at the end of the week for the scans, and we'll be in touch as soon as possible after that. Whatever it is, we can treat it.'

But don't you see I can't trust you anymore?

'You're being a bit enigmatic.'

'Yes. It is a bit enigmatic just now.'

There was a flatness about this comment that closed the conversation. I didn't want his interpretation anyway. Clearly, he had his secrets. I was getting the hang of it: secrets, codes, aggression – I was getting into the idiom, even if the tug of withdrawal was still strong. I nodded as if I understood him perfectly. Let him be cagey. On my way out I was given my appointments, and I exchanged the crutches for a stick. And now, I was thinking, there is no place for mystery on a busy London street. I am a man with things to do. I still have my plans.

It was the best of days. The air was light and the sky was a guileless baby-blue. As on the weekend after Helen left, I found particularities consoling. Uncomplicated perceptions: the steps down to the path along the river were of shallow stone; the sun fell through the overhanging leaves and reflected in dazzling ripples off the water. Lunchtime, and the secretaries returned from the sandwich bar, summer dresses flapping, now hugging thighs and buttocks, now billowing in the unpredictable breeze.

After a while fewer people passed. Fear nudged me, an impatient child becoming irritable, as if frustrated at not communicating its message. Its message was to run, to get out of reach, as far away as possible. For God's sake, it whispered, will you just sit here? Nothing else makes sense, it said, get out of reach. I have my plans,

I answered. There are appointments. There is a date to talk with Helen. I am a man with things to do.

But the image in my mind was of a chain of events: Helen, accident, hospital, illness – a chain of events like a linked Chinese dragon shuffling through the streets, its garish mouth gaping open enthusiastically.

IDEAS OF ORDER

The gate was of criss-cross metal, made to open like a concertina and slide across the exit. It had survived the decoration of the station. Its black paint, well scabbed with rust, was peeling off in stiff tongues. The car, having thrown me forward, followed as if to finish me off, but stopped just short, its radiator gritting its criss-cross teeth above my face. Lucky the road was soft. 'You got off lightly,' one nurse had said. 'What on earth were you dreaming about?' I shrugged and smiled ruefully, as if baffled. But where in the world would I be if I didn't dream? Always in the same place: lost in the city, wearing my body like an ungainly suit of armour. It's not possible. It's not possible to live that way.

I turned to find the ticket collector coming down the slope to his box at the gate. A skin disease scaled his angular, lizard face.

He smiled. 'Lovely day. Isn't it promising?'

I looked at him. 'Lovely.'

The first bench up the platform was empty. Words and names painted on the metal were fading and collecting dirt. Elbows on knees, hands blinkering my eyes, I composed myself, staring at the untidy swirls and ridges of dust on the ground.

Now is not the time for dreams. It is time to rediscover self-determination, and to impose some order.

Yet, when I looked up, Helen was standing next to me, hesitating before she spoke. 'Is this seat free?' Her long hair, worn loose, changing colour in the sunlight, covered half of her face as she looked down at me.

'Yes,' I said, 'yes. Yes, this one's free.'

She smiled at this response, and then before she sat down she slid her case between the seats, took off her coat and stretched as if exhausted, her arms straining outwards and then rising above her head. Her movements were simple enough, but she barged into my consciousness. It was the swing of her hair around her face, the shape of her arms, and the movement of her breasts beneath her shirt. The line of her chin was softened by an excess layer of flesh, which seemed to accentuate her smile. Her eyes met mine again.

'Have you been on holiday?' I asked.

She stroked her forearm, as if she might wipe away the tan. 'I only came home a week ago, my feet have hardly touched the ground.' She raised them and flexed her ankles, as if to demonstrate.

'Your ankles are white, did you wear socks on the beach?'

'They're not *white*, they're a subtle shade of brown.'

'Beige maybe?'

One nostril curled a little, as if she was not prepared to expend much energy on me. 'I do not have either beige ankles' – she crossed her legs on the seat and eyed me sharply – 'or a receding hairline.'

On the bench on the uncrowded platform, I remembered her words as we got off the train together: 'I'm not very good at new people. I thought it would take months to meet anyone.'

'So did I.' It was as if the train, the neutral ground between destinations, shortened the distance between us, so that when we left it there was a pact already established. 'You're too good to be true,' I said.

I stood up abruptly, and began to pace up and down, experimenting with not using my stick, stubbornly rehearsing my plan of action, composing myself.

Now is not the time for dreams. Let her think it's as straightforward as she would like it to be. Hi Simon, how are you honey? Hi sweetheart. Surprise her.

There was a pleasing quietness on the platform. The empty track shone in the sun until it curved away out of sight behind a grassy bank and a block of flats. At the gate the ticket collector was enjoying the day, leaning back with his eyes closed. He had the face of a basking iguana. His skin was like a map. I envied him his job, sitting unmoving as others hurried past, watching from behind his lined face, seeing people but not meeting them.

His eyes blinked open and met mine. I waited for a forked tongue to squirt out between his lips. Still no movement. I told him silently that I was only on the platform to meet someone, then I looked away. At the clock, back up the track, at the clock again.

The doors of the decelerating train opened in genteel unison. There she was. Helen. A face moving among the others at the end of the platform. She was smaller than most of them, hidden behind heads and shoulders. I saw her objectively for a second, an attractive girl, well dressed, that set expression which precedes recognition. I watched her before she saw me, and I had a sense of her too composing herself, adjusting her mood. So much the better. I went smiling to meet her. 'Welcome,' I said, as if I owned the place, and we kissed. My free hand rested on her shoulder, and our closed lips met briefly. Her hair was drawn away from her face in the ponytail. A sense of continuity. Lips slightly apart now, wide eyes with the habitual touch of gravity.

She said, 'Last week, I don't know how it happened. Were you very pissed off with me?'

'No, I didn't mind. I saw the others. Vince looks well.'

She smiled. 'Vincent's *thriving*.'

Her knowledgable tone was like a quick slap, to follow the kiss. I had no share in this familiarity, no right of way in her world, or any world so companionable.

'He's already thinking of starting his own business,' she said. 'He's full of ideas, Vince.'

She seemed to find comfort in repeating his name.

The ticket collector gave me a smile as we walked through, but I noticed too late to return it. It was an odd little smile that made me think he might prefer to meet the people who passed him every day. In his place, I would gladly hide behind my inscrutable face.

'But tell me about you,' Helen said. 'What did you do to your leg?'

'There's not much to tell really. A stupid road accident. One minute I was dreaming about my interview, the next minute I was in hospital. It was nothing.'

Mentally, another point chalked up: two lies already from Simon the liar. Our new relationship was defining itself.

We came on to the heath. The sky was a clear, flat blue over the shining grass. There was a sigh of pleasure from Helen. 'I've missed this.' She looked at me, and I was shocked. 'Oh God, Simon, let's be friends.'

She ran away, as if embarrassed, and I followed slowly. She wore a long, light jacket which lifted behind her as she ran, over tight jeans which ended above her ankles. I was shocked because I had suddenly recognized her. This was Helen. Her small face, slightly fleshy around the chin, her streaked auburn hair hanging down behind her, grown and cut and grown again since I last saw her, but unchanged. This was not the girl in my fantasies, this was Helen, re-entering my life, three-dimensional and human, revealing the absurdity of my plans. I felt foolish. I had had the idea of taking her for a drive, frightening her somehow, then dumping her somewhere, showing her my contempt, driving away, perferably in the rain, leaving her with miles to walk or hitch-hike home. It had seemed appropriate for the fictional girl I had in mind. Well, I thought defensively, all right, there are more realistic ways to hurt a realistic person.

I caught up with her. 'I just don't want to start off on the wrong foot Si. On your bad foot.' A half smile and an apologetic shrug. She was trying to find the right tone. 'You did mind when I didn't show up on Monday, on the phone you sounded so cool. You had a right to.' She put her hands in the pockets of her jacket. She was waiting for some response, but I wasn't going to help her out. 'It wasn't the right way to *do* it,' she said, 'to meet you again I mean. This is better.' Now she raised both arms, as if she had arranged for the heath to be here. Perhaps she had in a way, perhaps she had learnt some lines and picked on a place to say them. 'Don't you think this is better? There's space for us to talk. You know what I mean.' She let her arms drop to her sides. 'We're not strangers,' she said.

I nodded as if, after some consideration, I shared her positive attitude. I began to watch myself, cultivating caution, working on my own lines and consoling myself. The joy of a good plan is that it leaves no room for surprises.

At home we played cards. We were warming up for a conversation, spending words on trivia to find out how they sounded, and to beat new paths towards each other.

'It's your deal,' she said.

'I painted half of this wall,' I said, as I dealt the cards.

'I preferred it brown.'

'So did I.'

'It was warmer wasn't it.'

'You start.'

'All right. Give me time, give me time.'

We gave ourselves time, exchanging the words like cards, keeping them close and then extending them tentatively. She was just in t-shirt and jeans now, leaning forward to examine her hand. She looked up without moving her head, so that her eyebrows arched ironically. 'You said to me that you'd never try advertising.'

'Well I didn't get as far as *trying* it. How are your prospects?'

She put down her cards. 'Just fine. Twenty-two letters and one interview, my future is taking shape.'

From the house we moved back outside, into the garden. The midday sun made a difference. I lay on my stomach, my chin on one fist, plucking at blades of grass with my free hand, and watching her steadily. She sat comfortably cross-legged, a firmness in her posture. A magazine was open in her lap but she never turned a page, as if what she was looking at contained all that she needed to know. Her eyes wrinkled slightly in the reflected glare. Absently, she scratched an ankle. It took a physical effort not to move closer to her.

She saw me looking. 'What are you thinking?'

'I don't know,' I said. 'Thinking? Bad habit. What have you been doing?'

We talked jobs. She told me about a temping agency where she worked while writing articles and applying for various courses in her efforts to become a journalist. I suggested, as I had suggested before, that she ask my father to give her some contacts. She said it was a good idea, as she had said before. I told her about waiting for the Significant Thing. 'That's why those part-time jobs,' I said. 'Clerking, selling sale goods, filing hospital records, portering patients. I've realised – that's how I put up with a sense of drifting or lack of purpose, because I'm expecting the Significant Thing in my life to show up, the vocation.' The kick start, I added silently, which brings me level with the others, then allows me to outstrip them, on my beeline, unwavering, to some well-deserved destiny. My impulse was to take her hand and explain things to her, so that she could explain them to me. You *were* the Significant Thing in my life. Why did you have no faith in me? I would have loved to say something new to her, but that would be to deviate from my new plan.

To my surprise I sat up and took her hand, as if to shake it. There was no pain, instead a shiver, as if my hand was suddenly intensely sensitive.

'I need you.'

Matter-of-fact: '*Want* me. You just want me.'

I had no answer. The truth was not appropriate, the truth is overrated. I just watched her. She pulled a leaf from the bush beside her and rolled it carefully, as if for a cigarette. She put it in her mouth and chewed the end.

'Let's face it,' she said, 'you ought to face it, it's almost clinical. There you are with your degree, and your knowledge. I don't know, enthusiasms, skills, you've got your health and your friends, your stable background, money, I mean enough money, what more do you *want*? And you sit here, I mean you just stay here or you go out, but you don't *do* anything, you think something's going to fall in your lap, the meaning of your life is going to come knocking at your door like a double-glazing salesman. What is it with you?'

I had an answer to that, that was easier. 'It's lack of motivation, that's what the problem is, lack of motivation. It sounds puny when you say it, but that's what it is. I've got a place to start from I know, but that doesn't help. The future has no shape, you know that.'

She stood up suddenly, in her exasperation. 'I *know* that,' as if in disagreement, 'we all know that.'

I looked up at her, and nodded. A vague gesture towards her. We kept looking at each other, and eventually we smiled, at the comedy of our earnestness.

I made a large bowl of salad, very colourful, with carrots and peppers and cheese. Flurries of words. The words themselves seemed to be obscuring something, misrepresenting it like poor subtitles. We ate noisily, pushing the food around with forks until it could be neatly speared. We tried again:

'I was half expecting a gourmet production.'

'It's not the weather for it is it? It's a nice idea though, I haven't really made an effort for a while.'

'Maybe that's what you should do. Maybe you should be a master chef.'

I swept up a piece of carrot on a slice of pepper. 'I haven't the patience, have I? I haven't the patience for anything like that. I'm not a chef, I'm a cook. But I would like to make you something. When I'm in the mood I'll let you know.'

'Make sure you do,' she said.

This was safe territory: the indefinite future, the refuge of dying friendships. Then I surprised myself again.

I said, 'I went back to the hospital on Friday, for a bone scan.'

'Why did you need that?'

'It was just a check-up. What happens is, she gave me an injection of a radioactive isotope and then told me to go off for two hours and in the meantime drink as much as I could . . .' I told her how I had a can of Coke and a cup of tea, then found a pub and had a couple of pints, followed that with a fruit drink on the way back, and returned to the hospital desperate for a pee.

'She gave me this bottle and I went behind a screen, and it was so noisy against the bottom of the bottle that it sounded like a drum-roll, and there was this reeking smell of my piss filling the room. I thought it was going to overflow.'

I turned it into a joke. I exaggerated the amount I had to drink and I lied about the urine sample. I used the consultants' loo, which had a carpet on the floor and gleaming urinals full of cubes of disinfectant like so many sugarbowls.

She laughed, but she was not deflected. 'Why did you need a scan? Is there something wrong? I mean apart from you and me, you know, is there anything else? You're so tense. I'd want to be told if there was anything else wrong.'

I shook my head. No, nothing else. We have nothing to say to each other, isn't that enough?

The policing voice echoed: enough.

'Yes, I'm just tense, I think.'

But content all the same. It was going, more or less, smoothly. It was interesting to flirt with the truth, bait her curiosity, and still resist telling her what the doctor had said, and *proving* that I needed her. I wouldn't have her back on the strength of an accident of illness, that was the trump I was going to withhold. It wasn't difficult after all, to be as cagey as the doctor.

I took the plates away, into the kitchen. I had cleared up most of the mess from the salad as I made it. Now I tidied the rest of the bits and pieces and put the plates in the sink, splashing myself as I ran water on them. I watched the needle slide into my skin, and felt the cold fluid enter my blood.

She came into the kitchen and reached around me to turn the tap off.

'Come on,' she said, 'let's go outside again.'

As I turned round she kissed me on the mouth. Her hands were on my forearms, to stop me from holding her. There were inches of space between her body and mine. Her upper lip moved a little way between my lips. This kiss was her most eloquent statement, avoiding the unreliability of our words: so much, no further. New boundaries were being drawn. I smiled as our lips parted, and she took it as an acknowledgment, but I held her as she began to move away, my hand went up to her neck beneath the tail of hair and our feet shuffled, adjusting themselves to the etiquette she was imposing. I wouldn't let her move away, but she kept her distance. We moved together, out of synch.

'Shall we dance?' I said.

'There's no room to dance.'

'Do you remember what you once said?'

'What did I say?'

'You told me that when I came it sounded as if you'd stepped on my toes.'

'One long gasp, quite suddenly.' She pulled away as my grip slackened. 'Let's go outside.'

I watched her go. She was not prepared to be drawn into the past. Fair enough. The past was not my main interest either, for now.

In the garden we retreated back into banality. We compared tans, elbow to elbow, skin touching skin, as if we were about to arm wrestle. As if by prior arrangement, we resolutely ignored memories of our first meeting, her tanned arms the pretext for a conversation. I told her I intended to go to Paris, and she sounded enthusiastic. She said she would visit, and I promised to be sociable. Empty exchanges. We talked about my family and hers, our friends and what they were doing or intended to do.

The afternoon stretched until it became languid. Tension ebbed and silences lengthened comfortably. To preempt any more carelessness on my part, I allowed myself to tell her in each silence a little more of what the doctor had implied, and of what I had felt. The shadow of the tree in the neighbours' garden was stalking us as I told her about the C.T. scan.

I lay on my back and stared behind me at a mobile of paper cubes and diamonds. The empty room crackled: 'We're going to move now.' The table slid backwards, passing me under an arch which tickered quietly as it gazed at my torso. A camera in the corner moved with me. 'Fine. Now we'll go back again.' My upper chest was positioned beneath the arch. Above me, the angular shapes danced in their restricted pattern. Here at least, I was thinking, there is order. 'Hold your breath.' I held it, and a cross-sectional slice of my chest was filmed. 'Breathe again.' Inch by inch my chest was explored while the camera followed my progress and the stern disembodied voice gave its instructions. 'Hold your breath . . . breathe again . . .' Finally, when my chest and leg had been scrutinized, the voice stopped, the door opened and, like the Wizard of Oz appearing to Dorothy, a small mousy-haired radiographer entered the room. 'Thank you,' she said, 'you were very good.' 'Is it too early to ask what it looked like?' She laughed. 'Patience is something patients learn.'

As I lay on the grass, my thoughts followed the same path as they had during the scan. I used to visit an old lady who talked with a proprietorial air of 'it'. It had given her aggravation last week, it was not bad today, or not good. It was like a constant companion for her – she probably chatted with it when she was alone. You see, I told Helen, that was her, not me, I don't own any illness.

'I'd better go,' said Helen. 'It's time I went.'

Now, I thought, with tiredness rather than pleasure, it's almost time.

Buttonholed by memory again: at the pond we threw stones at the ice and listened to it resound like a metal drum. Very late one night, everything was white and silent, and the air was achingly clean. I walked a few steps over the ice and, to Helen's delight, cracked the surface and sank in slow motion into the shallow water and the freezing mud. I came wading out and chased her awkwardly across the flawless snow, but after a few steps we stopped, because it was too quiet, and the surface of the snow was so smooth, it seemed a crime to spoil it.

At the pond I asked her, 'Shall we have a coffee before you go? There's somewhere that's just opened that I've been wanting to try.'

We sat on stools around a small table. The place was all chrome and white surfaces. Helen said that since it was uncomfortable it would probably become trendy. She held her coffee in both hands, cautious again, sensing something.

'All right,' she said, making a joke of it, 'what are you thinking?'

I was abrupt, no humour in my tone. 'Are you going to tell me why you left?' I mean it has been on my mind now and then.'

She looked resigned, lowered her head to sip her coffee, looked up. 'Don't tell me you don't know, Simon. You *know* how I was feeling.' That surprised me, but I didn't show it. 'It was going wrong Simon, it wasn't going to get any better.'

'No better? What, you can tell the future?'

As planned, she was caught off-balance by my change of mood. 'I could tell *our* future. You weren't looking for anything any more were you? It was as if you had everything already.'

I allowed my anger to escalate. 'I was waiting for this – it's my fault, yes? That's what you're saying. There was Simon, simple Simon, thinking everything's going fine, then you decide to leave, and it's *my* fault. Yes, that's logical, that makes lots of sense.'

70

She shook her head. 'Don't be angry, there's no point in being angry. Don't spoil it, Simon, that's all I'm asking.'

'What is this 'it' I'm not supposed to spoil?' I thought immediately of the old woman, and the 'it' that began to rule her life. 'Is it some fragile thing we shouldn't touch?'

'You *know* what I mean.'

'Stop saying that. Because if it is so fragile, perhaps it wasn't so special in the first place. Did you think of that?'

'No Simon, I didn't think of that. You don't mean that.'

'Will you stop interpreting what I'm saying? You haven't got sole rights to this past you're talking about.'

Her voice rose in pitch. 'I just don't want this bitterness. It's no help. It's not a question of anybody's fault. You're still not the Simon I knew, can't you recognise that?'

'And how about old Vince? Is Vince the Simon you knew?'

'What do you mean?'

'I mean are you fucking Vince now?'

'What gives you the right to say that?'

Her shout rose effortlessly above the low sound of conversation in the coffee-bar. There was more than outrage in her voice, there was pain, I had really wounded her. Conversations stopped and heads turned. She looked around, suddenly aware that she had stood up to make her point.

Didn't I say she'd make an exhibition of herself in the end? She was never more than an amateur at hiding her feelings.

'Don't get angry,' I said, 'it's no help.'

'What gives you the right?' She interrupted, much more quietly now, as if she was talking to herself.

She looked at me, stricken and pissed off at once, then she picked up her jacket and left. It was over too quickly. I ordered another coffee, casual as you please, and while I waited I wet a finger and cleaned off a ring left on the table by the last cup. Smooth white surface. I looked closer and saw that it was marbled, veined in grey, like a network of cracks just waiting for the moment to splinter and give way.

Standing in the garden that night, where we were lying that

afternoon, I found no sense of satisfaction in myself. My mood was subdued, my emotions seemed to elude me, gliding out of reach. Only coincidence could pin them down, the sharp touch of serendipity triggering some clear response. There will be another man feeding the birds on his roof, I thought, I will see another flower-van, receive another unexpected smile and greeting.

Tired of looking inwards, I looked up at the sky. I could find no orderly constellations, only a great spray of lights like the lights of a city in darkness. No pattern. No chance of any pattern outside the hospital. The doctors might shape my future for me. Still, I thought, now Helen is marginalised, surely I can see more clearly? My next move at least is clear. My aunt is still waiting, still waiting patiently for me to visit her. But all I really wanted was to stay there in the garden, in the cool air, lying on the reliable grass, indefinitely.

IN MY COUNTRY

The thing is to build some momentum, and maintain it.

It was early evening when I set off, moving through a corridor of pink streetlights, under a grey sky, into a traffic jam. Stopping, starting, inching foward. The city clung to me. I wound down the window and draped my arm over the door, fingernails irritably tapping the metal. The driver on my right was in high spirits, as if he was somewhere else, gazing at the sky and mouthing the words of a song. Happy to my Grumpy. He saw me looking and stopped singing, Bashful now. It gave me a petty sense of satisfaction. 'Maungy old bastard,' said Steve. 'What's your problem?'

Steve's voice was his high. 'Look,' he'd say, 'Listen. Understand me, understand me.' He'd chatter away, I'd be in the passenger seat, one eye on him and one on the road, and he'd be chattering away gesticulating with both hands like he was conducting, looking at me to see if I'm getting the point, if I'm hearing it the way he wants me to hear it, and I'd be nodding and listening, inserting the odd word, always listening to him, and somehow we'd never quite hit anything, although we came close enough: a few swerves and emergency stops, and a spreading wake of angry motorists behind us.

Today he was in the passenger seat with me at the wheel, but he was as garrulous as ever.

'Explain it to me, what is all this shit? When are you going to grow up? You've got mum and dad worried, you know you have, and even Sammy knows something's up. You send me a letter that I can't read and it's in code anyway. You drop great hints like pieces of paving from a great height – 'Don't mention Helen' *crash*, hint. Why not? Helen, Helen, Helen. She left you, I understand. Is that it? I mean is that all? A little heartache gives you the right to cause panic in the Hare household? Harebrained, like I always said, and selfish, which is worse. I can't say I blame her. I thought you grew out of this sort of thing years ago.'

Steven never had a problem with verbal cowardice. It didn't matter what the situation was, he had the words for it, enough words to stock a library. He'd have plenty to say about my confused, confusing little letter. He got my share of words and I ended up, as he said, tight-lipped.

Traffic and buildings were thinning. Traffic lights still stuttered my progress, trying to slow me down, but it was too late – the momentum was there: once you're in a car you're already halfway to somewhere, even if you don't know where it is. I stopped again and watched clouds gently shoving each other behind a row of houses. One broke free and crawled along the top of the row alone, like a huge slug.

And now the road ahead was empty. It was like the beginning of a race.

Steve's letter was in my pocket unopened; when I moved I could feel its shape against my thigh. It had been waiting for me in the flat, a pale blue airletter, alongside the one from the hospital telling me that the biopsy was in four days time. Two days now, since the letter was two days old when I found it.

And now I raced into the empty road, changing gears, flicking on headlights, adjusting heat, turning the radio on. My mood shifted as I shifted gears: a sense of relief, a things-aren't-so-bad feeling, entering me like new energy. I am in control of my environment at last, the city is receding behind me, music is urging me away. The secret is speed, not stillness. My driving will measure out the night, beating time, racing ahead of it, confusing it. I am halfway there already.

Where? To my aunt's house, in search of an epiphany. Surely, short of a Resolution, or an Answer, I could find that much, some minor, illuminating insight? I felt my aunt was to blame. She created my vision of the future, and now it was up to her to adapt her stories to suit my present. Somehow money was made, somehow children were made, but the substance of adulthood was a story of my aunt's – an adventure in America, a trip through

Egypt, a cruise on an ocean as wide as the sky. When cynicism intruded on these stories and erased them, nothing followed to replace them. Helen marginalised, the Significant Thing a myth, Mr Pock cheering on my bitterness; nothing but a sense of vacancy. So the stories must be adapted, I had decided, for the late eighties, for my late twenties, and for the future. Otherwise how could I live?

My plan was vague. Aunt Molly's house was to be a signpost pointing foward, I would pause there and then keep going, keep going so that I would spend tomorrow night in some little pub in the far north of Scotland where there would be a loch with a monster and the pub would be so small that people would look round and stop talking when I came in. They'd all stare: where on earth did he come from? That kind of strangeness would be welcome, would be a welcome probably, a preliminary to friendly questions and conversation. Losing a few degrees of temperature on my way north, I would gain a few of human warmth, discovering a lodestone inside me – a breath of fresh air and I would be gregarious. And no one gets ill in those places. The things about those places is that they don't change.

I found the motorway, or the car found it. I was as mechanical as the pistons and gears, barely looking where I was going. I wound the window up, closing myself into the body of the car. It could be hard shell, through to the middle.

As the last light faded the rain began, but reluctantly, as if afraid of the dark. It shivered out of the sky and the wipers squeaked across the windscreen, smudging my vision. The car was like a boat leaving dock, the rope sagging into the water as it moves into the middle of the huge, dark lake, where there may be creatures below, and the rope is dangling coyly into the black water. I am not adrift, I am moving solo over the water, it is just the rope, dangling beneath and behind me, as if nostalgic for the bank, that slows me down.

A hundred miles, and a junction sent me directly north. My precarious sense of relief was fading, and as I started up the new road I decided to stop at the first service-station. I turned the radio off and wound the window down again, to listen to the wind battering the side of the car, and feel the rain spitting at the side of my face, as if trying to turn me back.

The sign said knives and forks, petrol pumps and wheelchairs, 1m and 31m. I imagined a million knives and forks, thirty-one million petrol pumps and wheelchairs, forming an avenue disappearing like streetlights into the far distance. The car slowed down quickly and noisily on the short slope up to the service-station, and the trees led me round to the carpark. It was very quiet in the middle, an empty lake. I switched on the interior light, so that the dark outside crept closer, like insulation. I took out Steve's letter, tearing it open as if I had always intended to do so at this particular moment, finding him addressing me as if he really was in the passenger seat, offering an alternative to the lakes I imagined.

Simon,

Where do you get your impressions of Malawi? Kipling? We live in an ugly breezeblock effort in a kind of compound near the university. We don't live on the lake and it's not 'my' lake, it takes up a big chunk of the country. The main thing to remember is – nothing ever happens here. When we're not working it gets pretty boring. I mean *nothing* ever happens here. I got the impression you were bored, but you should try it here. You can guess it's not exactly the ideal place for Daniel. Jabs or not the cholera is frightening. I don't think you can see straight from where you are, your perspective is a bit cockeyed.

Still, things have improved of course since Mum and Dad's arrival. They're really well, especially Dad. Isn't it great how he takes to retirement? I was worried about him when it happened, but obviously no need. Yes, they've both become grandparents, since they arrived, if you know what I mean. They're crazy over Daniel, and he's lapping up the attention naturally. I can't wait for you to meet him. We're trying to get him to say your name, 'Si-*mon*?' like that. 'Sammy's well too, wandering around permanently wide-eyed. I gave him a pith helmet for his birthday and he looks a hoot. You could still send him a card. We're all going on a mini safari next week.

And on top of it all, I'm watching Ally get on with her in-laws. It keeps taking me by surprise. It's a shame you can't be here but we'll meet soonish because we're going to be back definitely when the contract is up, which is early next year, and sooner if possible.

Now I'm running out of space and I haven't said anything about your letter. Look I'm really sorry about the thing with Helen, I liked her a lot, but, I don't know, B U T take it easy, don't indulge yourself like this, it's not the way is it? Sorry, I don't know what to say, I need to speak with you. But send me another letter, make it clearer, less enigmatic this time. O.K? *Please*.

All right, be seeing you, stay cool!

lots of love, Steve, Alice and Daniel xxxx
P.S. How was the interview?
Yes, how did it go? Why not ring us? Thinking of you, Mum.
Praying for you, Dad.
Wether is here, wish you were bewtiful! Sam!

I didn't know quite what to think. This was not the brother I was expecting, one who would plunge into my letter, berating and bullying me with his older brother common-sense. This was a family man, with news of his family and mine. This was a perspective I was not prepared for, one which diminished my problems to a matter of self-indulgence to be addressed swiftly and tactfully in the last few lines. There was a failure of understanding involved, one of us had no sense of proportion. Steve or me?

I got out of the car and breathed the sweet air. The atmosphere inside had become stuffy. Crossing the carpark, a very family orientated memory came back to me. Mum was holding my shoulders while I threw up, possibly on this same concrete, she was muttering advice, something like 'Don't get it on your shoes.' Out of the corner of my eye I saw that she was watching Dad and Steve head for the restaurant, and I felt a wave of self-pity at the sight. Nobody felt sorry for me.

I limped to the building now, as though dragging memory like an unwieldy ball from my ankle. Tonight I was driving, not riding.

Self-determination was still my aim, which was supposed to rule
out omens and memories, but the place had not changed. It was
still outside time, still an odd mixture of intimacy and boredom.
There was a couple talking in whispers, and there were three
individuals, none at adjacent tables, nursing coffees. The girl
behind the till was talking to another customer, addressing him by
name and asking after his wife. The man cleaning the tables did so
with an air of superiority, because he wasn't going anywhere, and
wasn't sleepy. I caught hold of the lines that had been trickling at
the back of my mind:
> It isn't really anywhere
> It's somewhere else instead!

It was the motorway, and especially the service-station halfway up
the motorway, straddling it, squatting on it and feeding it. I looked
around, wide-eyed. What on earth am I doing here? How can I
trust myself when I can land up somewhere like this? Not part of
the plan. The plan is to move, to not lose momentum. I left.

The brightly lit, entirely empty petrol station was a painting by
Hopper. The light crouched under the roof, afraid of the dark. The
pump groaned sleepily, the figures flicking across its face like the
dollar-sign eyes of cartoon characters. I expected to pay through a
grille in the window but the shop was open and I went in to see
three people, two boys and a girl, wearing green overalls and sitting
in a row behind separate cash tills. They were talking as I came in
but the middle one stopped and looked straight at me and said,
'Good Evening Sir!', like that, as if he'd been looking forward to
seeing me. I also got a 'Thank You Sir!' and a 'Good Night Sir!' and
as I left they all started talking again, they were having a Good
Time! I felt that later they might put a record on or a video and get
the booze out or the joints, maybe lock the door and get down
behind the counter and have an Orgy!

I left the scared light behind, cravenly hugging the forecourt, and
plunged into darkness. The thing about Steve of course, for all his
style, is that he doesn't plunge anywhere. He has codes of
behaviour, and willpower. He has plans that he carries out: I'm
going to get a job abroad; we're going to have a baby. You can
actually see him, in retrospect, building his life in a series of

premeditated moves. Steve doesn't plunge, he builds. Occasionally I overtook gaudily lit lorries, huge roaring autonomous things – that's Steve, slowish but more or less unstoppable.

I lost them when my junction finally rolled up and I slipped on to an 'A' road and slowed down to sidle across the moors. Now the dark crowded around, spilling over the shovel of light I pushed ahead. I remembered dry stone walls and cottages and milling sheep but it was all lost in the night and for a moment, unreasonably, I was scared. I was off my territory here. Yet each unexpected turning was familiar, as the old route spooled out like a ball of string. I remembered more than a cloud of birds on a snow-covered lawn, and my aunt's chain of misleading stories. Things I hadn't seen for a decade were still landmarks, caught momentarily in the headlights like snapshots.

The road I wanted was in a suburb, a nice area with tame, trimmed trees and well-kept gardens. I remembered red, white and blue roses leaning over the pavement, but they were all black tonight, as if in mourning. It felt wrong to creep down the quiet, dimly lit street after the hustle of the motorway, but it was all the same trajectory and I was still hoping for a fruitful visit, some sense of resolution, until I parked and got out of the car and found that the house was singing.

Perhaps only the half-darkness made it seem familiar, but I instantly recognised its well kept garden, its big grey face and the wooden gates hooked back in front of the paved drive. Time was being tactful, leaving the outside unchanged, doing its work behind closed doors.

It was not just singing, it was roaring. I had been planning to beg a telephone call, start a conversation, engineer a tour of the house, talk about the past. The house was to provide the clear slate I was after, the end of a chapter, a stepping stone. I don't know what I planned, but this wasn't right: somewhere else! had someone else! living in it. I walked up to the front door, through the flowerbed since the drive was crowded with cars. After the rain the smell of the mourning roses was heavy and too sweet. The door was opened by someone wearing underpants and a stupid grin.

'Gottabottle?'

'No.'

'Pssoff then.'

'I know someone . . .' but he had gone.

Cautious, I crossed the threshold and shut the door. The music was in control. It seemed that it was the music smelling of smoke and bodies and the music pushing the girl stumbling out into the hall.

'What's going on?'

It was the music she was asking. I climbed the stairs and opened the first door. The sex room. 'Close the fucking door!' – even the door was at it. A big double bed was monopolised by one couple, and another two were symmetrically busy on the floor on either side, moving in time to the music from the room below. Wait, a third person on the double bed was appearing from beneath the covers, tousled and large eyed, like a dreamer waking; when she wakes all the couples will disappear. Auntie? Not a sign of Aunt Molly 'Close the fucking door!' in here. A smile for the queue outside the loo, and then the next door. Video room, an audience of fifteen in the small spare room where I used to sleep, chorusing lines with the characters as if hypnotised. I know this film, I speak a line with the rest, Simon Chameleon, fitting right in. Door three, the dope room, fragrant and almost quiet, I actually got a smile as I looked in. Dreamy religious instruction in one corner, 'It's so obvious really, I mean it's so obvious.' I returned the smile. No, Yes, No, But yes, in the corner, and out again down to the kitchen where ice-cubes littered the floor, the fridge was open, glowing like a tv, an egg was being broken on someone's head. 'Fucker!' he shouted, stretching the second syllable like a battle-cry. The back door was locked, and I couldn't see the garden through the patterned glass. The two main rooms? The music was a physical thing, in control, no chance of overcoming it. I didn't bother to look.

That was the visit on which I had pinned my hopes. There was to be no epiphany at Aunt Molly's, no sense of the past recaptured or the future revitalised. Nothing so tidy. Just a continuing what-on-earth-am-I-doing-here sense of finding myself in the wrong place. I felt I'd set off without warning, travelled at random and landed up nowhere in particular. Mapless, clueless motion, as if the music or the video or something equally mindless was in control of me too.

I left, taking the smells of the garden and of the party back into the car, where they dissolved into mustiness, until an open window washed them both away. I regulated the heating and altered a ventilator so that it blew straight into my face. I didn't use the mirror until I was a safe distance away.

The meter was beyond its five hundredth mile when I took my foot off the accelerator and moved on to the hard shoulder. I rolled on, sixty, fifty, forty, until the last of my momentum was exhausted. All I need do, I told myself, is consult the map. I turned on the light, outlining my small environment, close and vulnerable, stuffy and uncomfortable. On the back of the Road Atlas was Britain, with Thurso perched on the edge of the sea. Isolated surely, a place to which to retreat. I looked in the index for it and found a great mass of black scribbling which I couldn't focus on. I thought it wasn't in the book, I thought 'o' came after 'u', I thought there was more than one index, I thought the characters had ceased to mean what they used to mean. It's somewhere else instead, there isn't any other stair any other stare, only eyes on the road, green and red, yellow and white, like the flower van, not to be run over or they'll burst, and monsters in a narrow motorway river, the River Motorway
Thursgill
Thursley
Thurso
Thurstaston
Thurston, Thurstaston, Thurso. Thurso. My motorway leaned over to the left and died just before it reached Scotland, so close, drained thin and red across the border and on p. 45 a profile of a huge white pointed head veined in blue stared at the edge of the page, threatened to turn and stare out of the book straight at me, no other stare
Quite like it.
Thurso, Scrabster, Olrig, Loch Shurrery (no monsters), Thurso Bay (sounds like a seaside resort). Perhaps the train should take the

strain. I think I fell asleep but not for long, I got out of the car, jumped over the fence and started walking away. It was cold and fresh and not as dark as in the car. It was the oddest feeling: I didn't know where in the country I was, the motorway was occasionally audible but was soon behind a rise in the ground, the sea probably wasn't far away, nor was Scotland, a couple of big cities were nearish, but it was all invisible. There was a bit of moon, some wispy clouds, thousands of stars, me and the grass and the smell of the grass.

I was a bit scared again, for no reason at all. I didn't seem to have any identity here was the reason. England doesn't usually have big, sprawling darkness and no city ever has it, but I felt lost here, drowned, but not drowned – it was more diving than drowning. I hoped it was more diving than drowning. Self-determination: driving, not riding. From here, I was thinking, the next step is to build, as Steve built. Well then, a few breaths of air and I have regained some kind of stability, glimpsed some kind of plan again. Onwards then, on up to the furthest corner of the map. I was still walking away from the car. I stopped. I stood still, waiting for fear to catch up with me. Breathing the cold air. Feet sinking into the soft earth. Unblinkered.

The country unrolled unmysteriously on all sides. My thoughts unrolled too, with a physical tremor, like a tight fist unclenching. A quick breath, and then some slow ones, as if a restriction had been removed from my chest. A gradual, tingling awareness of my body. Responding to a sudden urge, looking around like someone with evil intentions, I unzipped my fly and began to piss into the earth at my feet. A smelly, yellow, steaming stream, marking out this patch of ground as my territory. I smiled at myself. How long since I smiled? Mr Pock might not approve, but little Mr Pock, snuffling among his possessions and nursing his grudges, would be dwarfed here. It was in the dark corners of the city that he gained stature. In the middle of the night, in the middle of nowhere, cold, smelling urine and grass, a sense not of resolution, but of release.

Dawn soon, and the new day also marked a new month. August. Where would I be, I had asked myself, at the end of the summer? My words of six weeks earlier were catching up with me. A nimble piece of work with the door snapped off the chain at my ankle, leaving the ball of memory bouncing around at the edge of the road. As I got going again I was thinking: age will liberate you if you'll let it. Where will I be? Time will tell. Nothing is concluded or confirmed, I left the motorway at the next junction, but something is new. Helen offered me friendship and I pushed her away; I rejected Vince and probably alienated my brother; I am about to spend time in hospital. But something is new: I no longer feel coerced. On the roundabout I passed exits heading West, North and East and took the Southbound route, back the way I had come. Running away has given me the choice to return. I do not feel like a gatecrasher, I feel at home. More is possible. My movements are precise now because I am exactly halfway to where I am going, because there is still the journey back.

The grey light was briefly noisy while I overtook a big, clumsy lorry. It was the sheep-van, rushing its docile cargo to the city. I moved ahead, unconcerned, surfing home on the forward wave of the rush-hour.

AUGUST

BLUE EARS AND A PERFECT NOSE

The room has shrunk.

A doorless partitioned cubicle. Nil by mouth. Next door snores, and someone talking through their dreams. Every hour or so footsteps, the nurse passes, her face appears. If she would come in I would tell her why I am still awake. She is my age, she would be sympathetic. She would sit on the bed and we would chat for a long time, taking our time. I long for this to happen. The hospital had provided a radically new perspective.

'Still awake?' As if overhearing my thoughts, she appeared abruptly. A navy blue dress with a starched white collar, a watch over her breast, a coffee-coloured face in coffee-coloured light. Short black hair beneath the white confection of her cap. 'Do you want a pill?'

'I don't think so, thanks.'

'Well try and get some sleep.'

'I've been trying.'

'Goodnight.' Turning, leaving.

'Goodnight then.'

Nothing to be said. I explained to her absence: I am unpractised at conversation, rusty when it comes to social intercourse. In the past I may have enjoyed the gaps between words more than the words themselves.

I listened to the traffic and said to myself: one more car will pass and then I'll go to sleep. The headlights came in the window and stretched bars across the wall by my bed. The sheets, I thought, were as stiff as the nurse's collar. More headlights.

In the flat I liked the curtains to be tightly together for most of the evening, so that no unruly crack of light could intrude. 'Here is my space,' I would say, pulling the shadow across the floor, starting the argument. For Helen the window was an eye, to be covered only at night. When she woke in the morning she would sit up in bed and pull the curtain open, as if to reassure herself that nothing outside had changed. At home during the day the bed was her favourite place to sit, propped up by pillows in the corner, the room on one side, the street and its almost perpetual stream of traffic on the other. 'Just so I know they're there,' she'd say, shrugging, not explaining who 'they' might be. On Sundays the stream would dry up, and she would look bereft.

Footsteps, a shape, the apparition of . . . a memory.

Helen enters, and takes her place on the bed. The curtains frame her view. I enter, and sit down. I am holding a newspaper. An established tension reasserts itself.

'We could go somewhere?'

She wasn't listening again. Something on the street had caught her eye. 'That women has a perfect nose,' she said. 'Very slightly pointed. That nose is an heirloom.'

I tilted my head a little and raised my chin, but she didn't see the movement. I followed her eyes. Now she was looking at the line of closed shops, and the windows of the flats above. I coud read her mind: in each flat two people, time passing, restlessness. Above the flats the sky, aloof and immeasurable.

In these moods, for days at a time, our relationship was compounded of intimacy and distance.

She looked at me. 'We *could* go somewhere. Is there anywhere good we can go?'

'Yes. I can't think of anywhere. We could stay here.'

I was slouched in an armchair, a section of the newspaper on my lap like an invalid's blanket. Helen sat nesting in pillows and cushions on the bed, leaning her head on the window, her face expressive, possibly, of some inner dialogue.

'I mean,' I said, 'it's not an afternoon for rushing into anything is it?'

She ignored this. 'There must be somewhere good we can go.' This sounded like a contradiction of something she had not said.

'Is it so bad here then?'

88

'I don't like this,' she said, her voice faltering.

I stood up and moved over to her. 'What is it love? I can't say anything unless you tell me.'

She shook her head vigorously. 'Don't say anything. Don't say anything.'

I held her as she leaned away from me.

'Sometimes it's as if the walls are moving in.'

I held her. 'You know what we should do? We should fly somewhere. Somewhere exotic and not come back.'

'No,' she said. 'No no no we shouldn't. That's exactly what we shouldn't do. You don't understand. That's what it is,' as if she had just reached this conclusion, and it clarified things, 'that's what it is, you don't understand.'

Something had happened which I had missed. She unfolded herself from my arms and from the cushions and stood up, walked across the room, walked back. She kissed me. 'I'm sorry,' she said brightly. 'Shall we just drive somewhere. It's the least we can do isn't it?'

I stood up. 'We'll just drive then, into town. Although I'd rather fly.' I was content, in fact relieved, to respect her privacy. I touched her face. When words failed us I always thought there must be a way of touching her face, or of passing my hand over it, which would explain everything, and bring a smile, and close the gap. Wipe that expression off your face. Magic. A pass of the hand and it's gone.

We were both standing there, very close. My fingers brushed her cheek. She nodded. I chose to think that that was significant.

An uncomfortable, wet April warmth closed around us outside, making the open air feel claustrophobic. Siesta-time, and no movement. We might have been sleepwalking.

Driving her car, I headed towards the centre. She mostly stared out of the window, an elbow on the door, picking at a nail.

'A gallery?' I said.

'Sure. A gallery.'

People began to appear. Empty streets sprouted bodies: people at bus-stops, outside shop windows, at tables outside pubs. Then people walking, alone and in groups, purposeful. Suddenly it was busy, and growing busier, and when we had parked and left the car we found we were on the way to a demonstration. A crowd was pushing past us and between us, so many people that we were all moving at a crawl, hustling in slow motion towards Trafalgar Square. It was an intrusion, and I felt angry with these people, because I had begun to forget that so many people existed.

We joined a steady stream crossing the wide road at the top of the Square. The traffic-lights changed as we crossed and a car began to nose forward, but it was ignored. Green, amber, red: the car growled impatiently and people kept moving past it. When we reached the pavement the crowd was even thicker, and we were pressed and pushed towards the steps into the Square. I put an arm around Helen.

'Are you all right? This isn't really what we had in mind.'

She shook her head. 'Look at them all.'

We stood at road level, watching the bodies shuffling around the base of the column, struggling for position near a stage covered with instruments. A pigeon was sitting on a drum-kit and, as we watched, a man came to shoo it away, and it flew up in disgust, above the canopy and out of sight. The man looked at the crowd, and then returned to the wings of the impromptu stage.

'Let's not stay,' I said.

'Why not? There's going to be a band soon. It's a good cause.'

'All these people,' I said. 'I don't like so many people.'

'Yes,' she said, 'I know. I just thought it might be more interesting.'

We shoved our way back against the stream of demonstrators, across the road past the same trapped, growling car, and up the stone steps into the gallery. Where it was cool and very quiet. The door was open, yet it was soundproof. A man took our tickets without looking at us. Attendants slumbered in chairs in corners.

The peace in the place was infectious. In each room we drifted apart and met again, walking slowly, pausing and walking on. Room after room was empty. The light was perfectly even, and everything was still. Outside there might be a riot going on, or a celebration. I began to feel that we might come out of the building to find that years had slipped by, and no one had minded our absence.

A leaflet I had picked up gave us a guide to the gallery, but we soon lost our sense of direction, confused by its fractured squares. After we had walked round a room we were no longer sure which way we had entered it, or which way to leave.

Choosing an exit, I turned to find Helen still looking at a picture, the first she had come to when she entered the room. For a minute I looked over her shoulder. A nude woman was lying on the grass. A young man in courtly clothes was watching her, but his gaze did not exclude us. Sunlight played delicately on leaves, and on his bright cloak. His sword rested nonchalantly on his shoulder. I was going to say something to Helen, but saw that she was engrossed. She was looking into the man's eyes, trying to stare him down. She took a step back, as if she thought he might reach out and drag her into the picture.

I returned to a painting on the other side of the room. It was a town scene, full of groups of people, at meals and at business, occupied in selling and buying, in games, conversations and fights. A family arguing over a fire where meat was cooking; an ugly innkeeper drinking from a flask; an aproned butcher kicking a dog; a Punch and Judy couple arguing in a window, watching over the scene. I looked at it for a while, trying to take in the detail, and then I turned to speak to Helen, wanting her opinion. It needs focus, I was going to say, any one of these things could be highlighted. What's the use of a background without a foreground?

She had gone. I looked across and saw only the picture she had been looking at, as if after all she had been lured on to the canvas. The air-conditioning hummed at me; dust floated smugly in the artificial draught. I left hurriedly, only to find myself in a room that looked familiar. I retraced my steps and tried another exit, hurrying through and then stopping abruptly. A darkened, warm room in which my breathing became audible. A small, dimly lit picture opposite me, encased in a heavy frame. Another exit, and a long narrow room, or a wide corridor, hung with paintings like trophies. I wanted to run down this one, but didn't think it was appropriate, so I walked quickly, listening to my footsteps on the tiled floor, and emerging into a room full of lively, jabbering violent children, running and pushing, pointing at pictures and laughing. An attendant stood in a corner and watched guardedly, as if shy and wanting to join in. A teacher clambered up on a chair above the commotion and tried to take control.

A little girl came running up to me, big eyes meeting mine.

'Are you a painter then?' She smiled daringly.

'No, no I'm not.'

She moved from one foot to the other. 'You look like a painter.'

'Why's that?'

'Because you've got blue ears!' She laughed delightedly and blushed, strawberry red, as she ran back to the safety of her friends.

As the teacher began to restore order I stole out, unnoticed. The next room was empty so I continued, round corners, through corridors, up stairs and down, through swing doors and through room after empty room. I stopped to ask attendants if they had seen her. One looked at me as if I had suggested something improper, another simply smiled, and shook her head.

I stopped finally beneath a windowed dome. I looked up, thinking I should shout her name, and that the acoustic properties of the dome would radiate the sound throughout the gallery. There was a movement across the corner of my eye. I ran towards it, veered left, and almost bumped into her – a tourist in loud check shorts, with a camera around her neck, 'Excuse me!' she said.

'I'm sorry, you're not . . . I thought you were someone else.'

'Do I look like someone else?'

She was fat and her shirt and shorts were in shades of olive and lime green. I tried to smile but found that I was panting.

'No but I've been trying and I've looked everywhere and I can't find her.'

'Don't get carried away, young man,' she said. 'You should have a rest. Why don't you go and sit by the front door and wait for her there. You never *really* lose someone,' she said, enigmatically.

'I can't sit still while she's gone. This place is confusing.'

The woman smiled. Her eyes almost disappeared between pudgy eyebrows and cheeks. She looked like a good witch. Her camera swung as she reached out a hand to pat me on the shoulder.

'I should be getting on,' she said. She waved the hand expansively. 'There's so *much!*' She walked slowly into the room I had run through. 'I hope you find your friend,' she said.

The words were like a charm. I turned round and she was coming towards me. We met in the middle of the room, and I closed her in my arms.

'I lost you.'

She was looking to one side, speaking to my shoulder. 'I couldn't stay,' she said, 'I felt dizzy. I had to find somewhere to sit down.'

'Why did you feel dizzy?'

'Why did I?' She wriggled slightly away from me. She looked as if she hadn't considered this. 'I don't know why I did. Perhaps I haven't had enough to eat today, it's been a frugal day. That's probably it. Do you think that's it?'

'No, I don't think so.'

'Well I don't know. Anyway you'll laugh at me if I tell you.'

I held her a little closer, to reassure her, but I felt her body becoming tense, so I relaxed my arms again.

'I couldn't stay,' she said. 'That's all.' Now she was looking at me, staring at me, and I suddenly felt that we were in the middle of another argument, and I was being asked to participate without understanding its grounds. She continued, 'I actually felt there was someone after me, following me, I know it's stupid. I didn't even know who it was. This is the silly part, while someone was behind me the picture was in front, so I was being pushed and pulled, it was throwing out hooks and pulling me in.' She laughed. 'Well, say something. You think I'm crazy, don't you? Don't you have anything to say?'

'I tried to find you. I must have been round and round this place twice.'

'And then I was lost, one room after another, I thought the walls were moving in and moving around and hiding the way out.' She was crying now. I kissed her tears, relieved to feel her skin on mine. 'Let's get out of here,' she said, pulling away from me. 'I feel like I'm being chased from one place to another. Let's get out.'

We left the gallery and walked back down the steps. Big Ben was chiming half a mile away, but I missed the number of its chimes. The Square was empty, covered in leaflets and litter. Empty cans bobbed up and down in the fountains. The pigeons had returned and were scavenging, flying up in a flurry of wings to land just a few feet from where they had started, by a crumb or a scrap of food. They steered clear of the stage, as if they thought a man was still hiding there, waiting to chase them away or throw a net over them.

I said, 'You're right, there should be more to say. I don't understand, is the problem. That's all it is. I want to understand.'

'We could write each other letters.'

'We should give up speech. We shouldn't need it.'

'Dear Simon . . .' she began.

'Go on. What would you write?'

She shrugged, she wasn't listening again, she was heading for the car. Her hand was limp in mine.

She drove home, too slowly in the empty streets. I told her about the girl I had met in the room full of children. Helen smiled.

'She was right of course,' she said.

'I have got blue ears?'

She still smiled. 'The painter.' I put my hands over them, rubbed a lobe and pretended to see a stain on my fingers. Helen watched me in glances.

Up the stairs to the flat. The papers were in rumpled piles on the floor. Unfinished cups of tea were by the chairs. She collapsed on the unmade bed as if she was exhausted. I sat beside her.

In a week or two they would play cricket again in the park. Last summer, watching it was something we had in common. We would sit on the grass if it wasn't damp, and wave at the players we knew; and the sounds of the ball on the bat, mingling with the occasional shouts of the fielders, were like moments in a conversation.

I drew the curtains and, irritably, she drew them back again, and then opened the window. '*Look*,' she said, gesturing out, as if she had arranged the view for me. It was an expansive sweep of the arm, like that of the tourist. I looked. The long evening was beginning and the moon shone faintly above the line of the shops, a keyhole leaking a sliver of light.

She lay down with her back to me, her face hidden. I moved my hand through her hair. 'Tell me what you're thinking.'

She laughed. Where in the world did that laugh come from?

'I'm wondering about all the people with perfect noses. Don't you think it must be a handicap?' She didn't turn round or pause as she continued. 'I think so. People would stare, wouldn't they, and whisper behind your back as if you were an outcast. I wonder what she does, that woman, on Sunday afternoons? And what everyone does, regardless of their noses.'

'Why?'

'*Why*. Why what? What do you want me to say?'

'Okay, forget it then, be mysterious. Forget I opened my mouth. What's actually wrong with you today?'

'Something has to be wrong with me? I don't know what you want me to say.'

'That's not *good* enough.' On the word 'good' my hand moved compulsively, I jerked her head around by pulling a fistful of hair. She cried out in pain. We looked at each other. 'I'm sorry,' I said. I looked at my hand. 'I don't know what I'm doing.' After a few moments, sitting up now, she spoke.

'Something has happened, Si, we've allowed it to happen. A stage has been reached and passed and I don't think there's anything beyond it. Do you see?' Her hands on my face. 'There's nothing in the future for us.'

I saw that she had forgiven me. I heard her say 'us'. I felt her hands on my face. 'Nothing has happened,' I insisted. I kissed her palm, moved towards her, parted her hair and kissed the downy nape of her neck. 'Sundays are dead days, that's all.' She began to move away, to say something more, but I wouldn't let her. My hands moved over her shoulders, and down beside her breasts, and down to her hips. She shook her head but her hands stayed on my face, touching the features. For a long time, this is all I remembered – I took it as a reconciliation. The relief, to feel this mutual awakening. When I lay beside her there was a moment's stillness, before she turned and, in silence, closed the space between us. The rising and falling of her small breasts. Responses at last. A bite wrapped in a kiss. Her long fingers moved over my

95

scalp. Fingernails. Within the familiar movements there was a new passion in both of us. Mine was born of optimism. I was beginning to believe that touch was more eloquent than language, that perhaps we were above the inhibition of words.

It was the last time we made love. On the following Friday she left.

I probed, in the small bare room at the end of the ward I probed cautiously, and found that I was already anaesthetised. There is no pain in this memory, just a great sense of surprise. That so much was said. Helen at the window, gesturing out, trying to make me understand, trying to find the words. Could I have ignored so much? Could I have believed that the space between us was really closed? At first I think I'm lying, marshalling the images and bullying the memory into a particular shape. But that is exactly wrong: it is only now that I am telling myself the truth. I ignored her, she said that the relationship was over, she cried in frustration because she couldn't make me listen, and I welcomed her tears. I could have told the future that Sunday, if I wanted to. I preferred not to hear and not to see. Natural enough then that now, in this small bare room, there is nothing left to feel. Now, from this perspective I recognise Helen's sense of isolation, and I recognise what was new in my feelings as I stood in the night near the motorway. I want to break down the walls around me.

In the morning the night-nurse introduced herself as Agnes and sat on my bed and made unhelpful comments while I tried painfully to shave my knee and most of my leg.

'It looks like a hairy sock,' she said when I had finished.

'I don't think I want to do this.'

'Piece of cake,' she said with an official briskness. And then: 'Honestly. He's going to take out what they saw on the x-ray and have a look around. The upshot is an inch-long scar to show your girlfriend.'

I told her I didn't have a girlfriend. I also told her what I had been doing since leaving college, I asked her what it was like to work at night and sleep all day, and I mentioned some film that was on at the time. She said her shift was over, she had to go, and I asked her to wait for a minute and help me do up the back of my gown.

A different nurse came a little later to give me the pre-med, an undignified jab in the bum. After that things are confused. A man in the ward was talking continuously. Sitting up I could just see the man opposite him who was saying something to his neighbour in, inexplicably, a whisper. What is he whispering? Does he have secrets to keep? Order and disorder, stillness and speed. Does he know a good place to go? A cleaner came and said she had one just like me at home. One what? Does this one have cancer too? And I asked her for a jug of water because my mouth was so dry, surely some water would be all right, but she said it was a shame but I wasn't allowed to drink and she showered me with endearments instead, I was her poppet, her sweetie, her love. I thought about Agnes, the warm colour of her skin.

Someone came with a trolley and helped me on to it and wheeled me out of the ward. It was a film sequence with a patient's-eye camera angle. Behind me was a black lady who was unreasonably big. Her vast breasts loomed above me like an overhanging cliff, and her huge smiling face looked down reassuringly into my eyes. Panning forward, the ceiling was running away from me, on either side nurses and doctors walked briskly past, not sparing me a glance, ahead was a white coat topped by fair hair. Was Vincent here then? I should have told him not to come today.

We pushed through swing doors above which were the words 'Operating Theatre'. It wasn't though, it was a waiting-room. I understood, possibly mistakenly, that the surgeon was just finishing off his previous patient. I was very uncomfortable, and moved from side to side, groaning. The black nurse, whose very shape was emitting waves of comfort, kept saying I'd be better off lying still. I heard the words and understood them, but didn't get as far as acting on them. Nothing left to feel? Then why this fear? More lies, more confusion of the truth.

A new arrival, brandishing a hypodermic. 'We're ready now,' he said. He raised my hand as if to shake it. 'Just a small sting.' I looked at the hand he held, then looked away as he pressed the needle into it. His fingernail in my palm seemed to discover new blisters there. He rubbed the vein which had gone into spasm. 'Try to relax. Count to five. It'll be over before you know it.'

But I knew all along, I said. I was only fooling myself. I knew months ago, before the end of the story.

SOLLY AND THE BOYS

Pushing apart and opening up, prying apart the tendons to make space to probe inside. Chipping out the bone and scooping out the tissue, raspberry ripple. Squeezing the tumour in tweezers, black cherry falling into a gleaming frying-pan, plink! like a coin. White and hairless, the limb is passive. Yes, it says, as it is sliced and explored. Yes, yes, yes.

My whimper emerged as a yawn.

'It's good news. They think it was just a clot.'

'Why?' The word means nothing, it is carried on the tail of my yawn, on the tail of my dream.

'Go to sleep. You don't have to wake up.'

My eyes began to open in response. Agnes. Her blue dress and shining watch. 'I like to see you. I like to see your face. Would you put your hand on my forehead? Because I like your touch.'

I think it took all night to say this much. She was tenderly efficient, gone like a leaf brushing my wrist. 'I like to see your face,' I whispered, slow motion to the space where she had been. Was it her? Was it Agnes or was it Helen? If I could raise my arm I might still find the right way to touch her face. I looked for her, and found that the partition had broken down. The room had expanded, for some reason my image was of a balloon blown up, I looked for her and saw other beds around mine, Agnes attending to another patient. I slept.

Hard to know when I woke up, hard to find a way out of sleep. A silent screen entered my dreams and left them and re-entered, faces talking earnestly without words. The smell of the starch on the pillowcase. The ache rising to a pain, and beginning to wake me as it had when I lay in the garden after the accident – a pain like a muted bell. Sounds. The last thing was becoming aware of other

99

people. The talkative man was on my right, watching the tv and listening to it through earphones, and still talking, as if he had never stopped. Opposite me the whisperer, on my left a man who was all skin on bone, like a crude puppet. Beyond them, around the room, six others.

'Are you awake yet?'

It was a nurse. Not Agnes, so it must be morning again. It must be Tuesday morning. She gave me a baby-faced smile.

'Are you awake? Welcome back. Wake up now, you can't sleep for ever.'

Now there was a thermometer in my mouth and her face above mine, too wide, too smiling. Now she had gone, and it was too late to get back to sleep.

I threw up my breakfast. The nurse told me I was 'anaesthetically naïve', and I nodded as if I knew what she meant. The phrase seemed perfectly just. All summer my eyes had been wide open but my sensations had been damped by numbness: something happened but the appropriate response did not happen, nothing was felt, nothing was taken in, as if all summer I had been suffering from the effects of a general anaesthetic, throwing up, unable to digest any experience. I looked around at my fellow patients lounging, and at the busy nurses. Then this should be a treat. Now is the time to recuperate, now when boredom is my worst problem and nothing is asked of me, because the conventions of the hospital cosset me. That morning I was x-rayed without even leaving my bed, in a sandwich toaster of technology. I spent the whole day failing to get back to sleep, waking up in a slow movement from detachment to involvement. The hospital gradually imposed its presence. There was not enough sound and there were too many smells, not the familiar good and bad smells of the house and the street, but smells of starch and disinfectant and bodies and institutional food. A faintly urinous smell. Sometimes the smell of vomit. Smells of drugs, sterile wrappings, soap and sweat. Stale air. I found little else to preoccupy me at first; I was living in an olfactory region.

By the end of the day I had woken up, and at night I couldn't sleep. There was an infection around my scar (*my* scar?), and Agnes had to take my observations twice. Blood pressure, temperature, pulse. The first time, she talked as she worked. She answered some of the questions she didn't have time to answer on the morning of the operation. Yes, she told me, she liked night-shifts, she liked the responsibility of being awake while others slept. As she took my pulse, her eyes on her watch, I admired her neck, and imagined her shoulders beneath her dress. Her short hair left her face and throat looking unusually naked. Naturally, I knew her smell. When she was close to me, it overcame the smells of the hospital; her flesh and her breath, a clean, natural odour beneath a light scent. Unbidden, my hand rested on the back of her neck when she leant over me to read the thermometer. Cool warmth. I think she winked as she moved away.

The second time she came, she sat on the bed to talk.

'It's good news about the haematoma.'

'Yes. Yes it is.'

'I thought you'd be more pleased.' She looked injured.

'I am pleased. It's good news.'

'You can't please some people,' she said.

'You please me. Just by being here you please me.'

She laughed. 'Aren't you sweet.'

I nodded. 'I'm a sweet man, but I'm starved of affection.'

'Doesn't anybody love you?'

'Nobody. It's because I'm not really sweet. I'm sour.'

'I don't think so. I thought you were sweet when you were chattering at me before your operation, and when you lay there muttering to yourself last night. I thought, this one looks like a sweetie.'

I looked around the ward. 'I bet you say that to all the boys.'

As if I had reminded her, she looked around too. 'I'm busy.'

'Are you? I don't see anyone needing help.'

She stood up and replaced the graph of my progress at the end of my bed. 'You'd be surprised the amount I have to do. I have a stack of reports up to here.' A hand level with the watch over her breast.

'When's your night off?'

'Tomorrow. Are you going to show me a good time?' She laughed again as she left.

★   ★   ★

101

By Wednesday morning I was less groggy. I discovered the window. I found that early in the morning I could watch a fruit stall being set up and doing business. Later I saw two politicians going into a winebar. And cars, all day and all night as long as I was awake. Straining my neck and my creativity, I tried to grant the driver of each consecutive car an occupation, a personality, motives and desires. It was an experiment with Helen's perspective, looking out of the flat. My world was peopled with conscientious, adventurous, ambitious and adulterous drivers. But they moved too fast for me, the lights changed or the traffic jam moved on and the character sketches had to shrink to destinations: office, home, wife, husband, lover, pub, restaurant, shops, another hospital, the North, the South, station, airport . . . and then, after lunch, this list ended too, my ingenuity defeated, and I was reduced to a string of names, as if naming people made them real, one after another, a telephone book of first names, like invitations to a huge party, a party like the one at my aunt's house, but bigger, with rooms to accommodate everyone's taste, even a room like the one I lay in now.

There were things to do, to prevent me from resigning myself to boredom automatically. For the first time in months I read a book, swallowed it in great chunks, a fat nineteenth-century novel. On Wednesday there were visits from the physiotherapist, and on Thursday there were my return visits, to the gym. In spite of Agnes's good news, there were more scans. Some of the tissue they examined was 'not quite what they expected'. The men on either side of me were not likely to become fast friends; the talker was engaged mostly in a monologue, the thin man was mostly silent, unless a nurse had time to talk to him. He was friendly with the nurses, and I decided that his condition gave him a lonely sort of ascendancy on the ward. Opposite me the whisperer grew quieter, as if his secrets grew more precious, but to compensate his breathing became louder, until it was audible all over the ward. A snort – a sort of audible wince, followed by a long faltering breath. A silence.

There wasn't enough to do. On Friday, the day before I left, I was making lists again, sitting up in bed with the newspaper

propped on my left leg fitting words into the margin alongside
Home News: helplessness, fear, anger frustration, boredom,
boredom, strangeness. I changed the order to make the acronym
Bbhaffs. I felt like an architect examining the structure of a house
he finds himself in, an ugly house, or an uninspired one. Perhaps to
examine it in this way is a step towards redesigning it. Fear came
second to bottom on my list, and strangeness last of all. Strangeness
had evaporated for me in the face of the ward's overwhelming sense
of order. There was nothing mysterious about it, life in the ward
was as carefully plotted as the graph at the end of each bed. On
hospitals I am like a teenager who lost his virginity long ago: it's
pretty crass to talk about it really, but endlessly tempting. I spent
half an hour silently explaining the ropes to an imaginary new
arrival, perhaps whoever was going to have my bed. The thing to
watch out for, I finished, is that you might find you are content
here, shaped by events for a while, with all pressure removed. On
the one hand it's stifling, but on the other, the absence of
responsibility is a consolation. He looks at me sceptically. I smile.

In the margin on the other side of Home News I began to write a
letter. 'Dear Steve' . . . I crossed that out and wrote, 'Dear mum
and dad' . . . then crossed that out too. I tried 'Dear All,' and it
seemed to strike the right unselective, encompassing note. I reread
Steve's letter, reminding myself of the accusations of self-pity
between his lines. Then I wrote:

Dear All,
    Nothing yet, nothing resolved just yet. But I'm picking
things up. I'm learning where rules don't apply. (Almost
everywhere.) I'm improving my powers of observation, or
trying to. Nothing else to say yet, although I recognise that
there's a lot to say. Be patient. That's another

I ran out of space in the narrow margin, and dropped the
newspaper.

Thousands of miles away, I was thinking, my father is praying
for me. Isn't there more to say to him? I've read the paper, I can tell
him about budgets, Middle-Eastern wars and sport. Keep him up

103

to date on the cricket. What was blocking me, I realised, was the need to write to Helen. As if all I had been waiting for was this realisation, I wrote to her, on a clean sheet of paper begged from a nurse, covering only one side, trying for a precise and uncluttered style. The limitation of space was a good discipline.

It was mid-afternoon. I had to check the paper again to see what day it was. Friday. I had been in hospital since Sunday night. Time had become viscous, syrup sliding from a spoon, stretching with the effortful ease of someone stretching their arms on waking. After I had written the letter time slowed down still further, until it reached a stodgy standstill.

'Sigh. Sigh? Ssss.'

'Whar?'

'Si? Ssvince.'

'Who?'

'Vince. Are you awake?'

'Vince.' In my mouth his name was like a shhh in a library.

'You said four-ish. I could come back.'

My eyes focused, but my voice remained unsteady. 'Vince. No, don't come back, I mean don't go. Stay.'

'Brought you some cans. Don't know if it's legal.'

'No. No problem.' I sat up, blinking and yawning. 'It's four-ish? I've been asleep.'

'I noticed that. How are you feeling, how did it go?'

'All right, I think.' I half turned to arrange the pillows behind me. 'I mean I don't know, they're not telling me. They don't know either. They say they don't.' I leant back and looked at him again. 'What are you doing in a suit?'

'I've come straight from work haven't I? You're my dentist this afternoon, do you want a look?' He opened his mouth and leaned forward, as if he was about to take a bite from my face.

And finally I was awake. Vincent. Vincent and Helen. 'Did Helen tell you? Did she tell you what I said?'

'She said you were a bastard and you were behaving . . . oddly, I think she said. Are you a bastard?'

'I was yes, I don't know why. No, I'm not.' I shook my head. 'I'm not now.'

'She had no idea you were going into hospital.'

'I didn't tell her.'

'Yes?'

'I mean I didn't want her to know.'

He made a sound, like a cough. 'Why not? Would you mind telling me why not? You were together for God knows how long, didn't you think she'd be interested?'

'We stopped being together didn't we? I don't know. I didn't want her feeling sorry for me, or doing anything for the wrong reasons.'

'There wasn't much danger of that.'

There it was again, the tone that left me guessing. 'What do you mean?'

'Well that doesn't make sense – 'do anything for the wrong reasons' – I don't know what you're saying. She just cares, that's all.'

'She's right, I was behaving oddly,' I said, trying to close the subject. 'Give her this?' I gave him the piece of paper, folded into an envelope. 'It's easier than trying to explain.' I might still have been talking sleepy gibberish for the progress we had made.

'Sure.' He put the envelope into his pocket without looking at it.

There was a silence, a mutual withdrawal, and he took two of the cans out of the bag. 'Too early?' I shook my head. 'Just right,' and he opened one with a 'fssh' of trapped air and handed it to me. Sound and smell and taste rolled back the sensations of the ward as the presence of Agnes had done before. I smiled as I thought of her. She was back on duty tonight.

'I don't get this,' said Vincent, 'you're looking better than you did in the pub last month. Food agree with you here?'

'No, I'm more relaxed. Just glad to see you I guess.' There was an intense pleasure in saying this, with a steady voice now, and no ulterior motives.

'You weren't glad to see me last time were you? What's changed?'

'You?'

He answered seriously. 'I don't think so.' That's when I remembered that I liked Vince, when he took my question

105

seriously. 'I'm one thing at work and another out of it, you know that, but I mean how far do we go back? We go back far enough.'

'So?'

'So you know I'm not going to change my attitude every time you turn around. So don't be more complicated than you have to be. Don't be paranoid.'

'Must be me then. Must be me changing.'

'That's how it seems to me.'

'That's funny, I thought it was everyone else. So anyway, all right, I'm more relaxed now. How are *you*? How's work?'

He laughed. 'What I like about you is you're so informative,' then he shook his head. 'Work's boring, tell you the truth I may chuck it. I may try something on my own, or on my own with friends.'

'That could be good.'

'Could be. Listen,' gesturing with his beer can, messy blond hair over his rosy, almost smirking face, he looked like the comedian in a low-life club. You always knew when Vince was about to tell you a joke. 'Listen, why doesn't an English student look out of his window in the morning?'

'Why?'

'Because then he'd have nothing to do in the afternoon.' He didn't wait for a reaction. 'That's you,' he said, 'that's been you ever since you left college. What you need is a job. What would you think about working with me? If I was trying something on my own?'

'With you? Shit, I don't know. I don't know if it's what I want. Small business. Entrepreneur? I don't know if it's me.'

'Yeah, I know. I don't know if it's me either. I'm just tired of working with people I don't like. I'm getting expert at being nice to people I don't much like.'

'You shouldn't do that. If you do that you're not, I mean you're speaking a different language. It's too confusing. You shouldn't do that.'

He misinterpreted me: 'Well don't worry, I'm not doing it now. Don't start getting paranoid. I like you enough to let you know when you get up my nose.'

He stayed for an hour and we talked continually, about my parents and his, my interview and his job and his plans, the doctors, even the films I wanted to see. We didn't talk about everything, but when we avoided subjects our sidesteps were neat and almost unselfconscious.

I asked, 'Do you see much of Helen?'

'I don't see much of anyone at the moment, that's a problem with the job. The Jester is a meeting place for everyone on a Friday, and we usually go on from there. I'll probably see her tonight, so I can give her the letter then. You should come back there, sometimes it's all right, sometimes it's a good place. Why have you been such a recluse all summer?'

'I've just drifted. I've either drifted or had useless spurts of energy that get me nowhere. I feel like I've come in here for a tune-up.'

Vince finished the beer and put the can on his knee, squeezing it in his large hand. 'Are you worried?'

I watched him crush the can, watched it buckle, dribbling beer on to his fingers below the knuckles, on to thick, soft hair.

'No,' I said, and realised that it was true. 'I was before. I expect I will be again.'

Before he left we arranged that he would drive me home the next day. I watched him go and then, after giving him a few minutes, peered out of the window, trying to catch sight of him. Was that him? A blond head was passing the fruit stall, but it was too far to be sure. There is in me an outward-looking consciousness, an outstretched hand, still there in spite of myself. I watched the blond head as it turned out of sight, towards the tube. Vince. Arthur and Elizabeth, Steve, Alice, Sammy, Daniel. Molly. Helen. Agnes.

Friday night. Although I hadn't seen her since Tuesday, Agnes hardly acknowledged me when her shift began, because she was busy at the bed opposite. I watched her movements around the bed, taking observations, using both hands to adjust the drip feed, bending over to tuck in a corner of the sheet while talking to the relatives. The shadow of her legs visible through her skirt. At first I just watched her, an unembarrassed voyeur, impatient for her to come and talk to me, but I slowly became aware of the man she was tending. It was the whisperer, but she called him Solly, and once I had heard her say it I realised I had heard his wife using the name too. I had watched him and his relatives on and off since I had come on the ward. It was a surprise when I finally realised how ill he was, because to me he had seemed quite healthy before.

When I noticed him on the morning of my operation I was lying flat and miserable and he was sitting up, bare-chested, talking to his neighbour. Thick grey curls on his shoulders and forearms. Peering over the blankets I had thought he looked robust, although his voice was so low. This image of health stayed with me, even as I improved and he declined. I was able to get out of bed and move around on Thursday, but by then he already looked too ill to talk to. He didn't eat much but he was often sick. Increasingly, he groaned in pain. He was very weak, and nurses had to help him sit up or lie down. Sometimes with other patients a nurse would be in a hurry or would exchange sarcastic remarks. Not with Solly. I thought at first they must be annoyed with Solly.

The thin man on my left looked like a skeleton with skin stretched over it. He was always in pain, and he had to have a special mattress to stop his skin from breaking around the pressure points. Tubes as thick as his fingers fed him and bled him. But he smiled and chatted with the nurses, and if people had trouble meeting his eyes, he didn't seem to notice. (I am thinking of myself, I had trouble meeting his eyes.) Solly's manner was, yes, grave. No irony in him. His whispers grew less frequent, and quieter. He was patient and angry at once. Always there was an edge of pain in his eyes or the corner of his mouth. But he was aware that there was no point in making a fuss. This awareness was so strong that he was apologetic and embarrassed about causing trouble for the nurses.

From Wednesday relatives were with him most of the day and much of the night. His wife came earlier and stayed later than any other visitors. She was a capable lady. She would fetch a pot for Solly to puke into, would demand that he was prescribed stronger painkillers, and would ask the nurses whether they were still serving him kosher food. Most of the time she just sat by him, not saying much.

His small wrinkled father in brown suit and hat visited as often as three times a day. It wasn't in any of them to show strong emotions but his father looked saddest of them all. He always looked surprised, as if his son had disappointed him. There was a teenage daughter, another daughter in her early twenties, and a tall man in a grey suit and hat who I took to be Solly's brother. There was room for no more than two at his bedside, and usually some would be at the foot of his bed, talking in low tones.

At ten o'clock on this Friday night the father and the wife were by the bed when the brother brought in another visitor. He was an old man who walked in slowly, looking around curiously. His back was bowed, it seemed by the weight of his thick white beard and his heavy black hat. Solly's wife made way for him and he sat by the bedside for about ten minutes, after which the brother led him away again.

The main lights were off now. Only the small red night-lights and a dim light over Solly's bed were on. Pain kept me hovering on the edge of sleep so that what happened around the bed opposite was like a dream, with the uneasy personal perspective of a dream. I didn't know much about it. I knew that in spite of my uneasiness I was glad to be there.

Solly could not sleep and moaned in pain like a child who cannot understand why he must suffer. He knew that there was no point in making a fuss but the pain was overcoming his own nature. His wife called Agnes, who brought more tablets.

'These are very strong, Solly,' I heard her say, 'what you need is a good night's sleep.'

There was impatience in her voice. Her job now was only to make him as comfortable as possible, and it wasn't even in her power to let him die peacefully.

Solly whispered his thanks, and the effort made his voice louder than before. 'I don't want to pester you.'

It wasn't long though before she was called again. She fetched a commode and found another nurse to help her remake Solly's bed. The wife, father and brother sat outside the drawn curtains and listened to Solly's whimpering. His voice raised again in frustration.

'My wife won't go away. My wife won't go away.'

'Do you want her to?' said Agnes.

'No.'

The curtains were drawn back and for a moment the relatives were sharply silhouetted as they stood at the bottom of the bed looking at the dying man. 'We're putting a special blanket on,' Agnes told the wife, 'because his temperature is very low.' Solly kept drawing up his knees and she kept asking him to keep his legs flat so that the blanket would stay close to his body. It was a dim silver in the light, like a padded sheet of foil.

I slept after that and when I woke the curtains were drawn around Solly's bed again and his wife was sitting alone outside, not moving, staring at the curtains. I looked at the pale green curtains around my own bed, which could effectively close me off from the rest of the ward. Useful for intimate moments with the bedpan, and for concealing bodies. Agnes came to speak to Solly's wife. I thought of Helen, drawing back the curtains irritably, throwing open the window on to the dark street and the silver sliver of moon. '*Look.*'

A little later two men arrived on the ward and stood at the door looking awkwardly at each other and expectantly at the nurses. Soon after, the curtains around all our beds were drawn. After a while I saw shadows move around the bed opposite, heard the sound of things being shifted and of men sighing with effort. Eventually all our curtains were drawn back again and we all sat up, those of us fit enough, and we had our breakfasts a little late.

Agnes found the time while serving breakfast to give me a kiss, because she knew I was leaving that day. A brush of the lips.

'Are you all right then?' I asked.

'Of course I am. Will you come up and see me some time?'

'I will. I mean I will if you wouldn't mind. It's what I planned to do.'

I couldn't read her smile, because it encompassed too much. I always stumbled on this silent eloquence, a gesture or a look which signifies more than itself. She smiles because she is pleased that I want to see her again. She smiles at my clumsiness. She smiles at my confusion, knowing that I don't understand her serenity. What is the correct response to a death? Is there an established etiquette? I had hoped for a sense of a secret, not shared by me – something I could guess at. Nothing, just this efficiency.

When Agnes had gone the thin man croaked his congratulations, in short sentences, leaving himself time for breaths.

'I'm impressed, son. Kissing already. Quick work.'

I shook my head. 'Thanks.'

'Make the most of it. I would if I were you. I learnt a new word yesterday. Do you want to hear it? Etiolation. It's my new word.'

'What does it mean?'

'It means I'm next.' He winked, and raised his emaciated arm eagerly, as well as he could, like a boy eager to be chosen for a team. 'Me next.'

'No,' I said.

'Yes,' he said. He looked at me steadily. He was all eyes, they were protuberant and bright, the only part of his face that hadn't shrivelled. Bulging like ripe fruit, so that it seemed unlikely that his lids would stretch over them. 'Sick?' He said. 'You want to talk about sick?' It was impossible to interpret his tone. 'Sick of it all, that's me. Sick in the heart. Which means sick of life.'

After breakfast the doctor stopped to talk to me on his ward round. 'I'm afraid I don't have any news,' he said. He gave me a date for an outpatients' appointment. 'We're going to have to keep you on tenterhooks I'm afraid. We haven't exactly come to any conclusions.' His bobbing tuft of hair bobbed around his eyes and he brushed it away. I felt quite relieved at his words. At least I can still spot a liar, I was thinking. I can't spot a dying man in a bed opposite me, but I can spot a liar. He changed the subject and asked how the physio was going, then changed it again, passing the buck unsubtly: 'Dr Hunt will be able to explain.' I bet.

I watched the thin man curiously, waiting for a last clue. Just before Vince came to take me home, he had visitors. His wife arrived, carrying their child. All smiles now. He held the chubby little boy up in his arms, inches from his fleshless face, and he opened his mouth to reveal outsized teeth, then opened his jaws to reveal a fat, wet tongue. Sitting up on my bed, in jeans and a pyjama top, I flinched, thinking that for some reason he was trying

111

to scare the baby. It was his wife who saw me, saw the prurience in my eyes and met it with an impatient glare, more scornful than angry. As I turned away, blushing, I saw the baby gurgling with delight as its father blew a raspberry between thin, smiling lips. I understood his tone earlier, understood that he had been mocking my earnest confusion. He was bored with the idea of his death and bored with the fascination and hypocritical tiptoing round the subject of strangers. The baby, I realised, understands. The baby does not see a frightening skeleton when he looks into his father's face, he does not see his own mortality there. The baby has no time for symbols or metaphors. Life is the mystery that he and his father are exploring. Death is an end to the mystery.

Things happened quickly. Vince arrived, I smiled at the thin man but he was too preoccupied to notice, and I said goodbye to the Sister. Downstairs I was given a ·card with my outpatients' appointment, and then we were out on the street, I had left my oasis of order and I was on the street I had been looking down on from my window. My observations hadn't prepared me for the noise of the cars and the people, the smell of the fresh air and exhaust fumes, the warmth of the sun and the cool advances of the breeze. I have already proved myself less perceptive than a baby, I was thinking, it must be necessary to start again. Building, like Steve, starting again. 'This way,' said Vince. 'Just round the corner.' And then we were the motorists I had been constructing stories for, Vince and Simon, and I was returning home conscientiously.

We parked in the little road behind the flat.

Vince said, 'I haven't been here for ages.'

'We should have stopped and got some food or something.'

He just smiled.

Inside I found the place cleaned up and the kitchen stocked with provisions.

'Helen used her key. She said she hoped you wouldn't mind.'

On the kitchen table there was a big bunch of flowers stuffed in a milk bottle. Helen's note was more concise than mine, a no-nonsense response: 'We must talk.'

'What do you want for dinner?' Said Vince.

★   ★   ★

Late that night. Voices surrounded me, as if there was a crowd of people in the room, each taking their turn to deliver their name. A dream of gregariousness. There were names I recognised, half familiar names, names I had never heard, including no doubt the names of Solly's family, of the thin man, the talker, the baby-faced nurse. Vince, Arthur, Elizabeth, Steve, Alice, Sammy, Daniel, Molly, Helen, Agnes, Solly, David, Louise, Anne, Tom, Belinda, Geoff, Glenn, Mike, Paul, Sally, Eddie, Ian, Graham . . . They were soothing in their unpausing flow, as the sound of a river is soothing, flowing confidently at its own composing pace. They were silent, but that was because I knew that I was dreaming. Whatever pace they were moving at was my pace too, they would still be there when I woke up, and then the silence would be broken. It was just a matter of waiting until I had finished dreaming.

THE BUILDING PROGRAMME

'What I can offer you,' said Dr Hunt, 'is chemotherapy, possibly radiotherapy, and surgery. After the knee replacement, after physio, there's no reason at all why you should have as much as a limp. No more hang-gliding, I should warn you, but there should be no serious limitations. I don't want you to fret. We're talking about an eighty per cent success rate in America. I don't want you to worry too much, it doesn't help.'

I know that Dr Hunt is not as important as he thinks. He is a sub-plot character. Two hours after I have met him he is half forgotten, because I am on my way to visit Helen, to make my peace with her.

Trembling on the edge . . . trembling on the edge of some-thing . . .

It's not me, it's the tube, shivering down the track, transmitting vibrations through the glass of the window, into my shoulder, through the muscles of my neck and into my face, down my arm and into my hand. The burnt hand is no longer burnt, not so much as a faint scar remains. There are no more excuses, I have no plans to fend things off. I am travelling on this train naked. No wonder I am trembling.

Picking up clues. The speed of the train is important; neither too fast nor too slow. I thought I had either to drift or to race along some semi-charted course, I thought there was no other choice. But I am learning self-control. I study the patterns of dirt on the window, the grey-brown crust neatly arranged around the edge of the pane, and I consider the letter I have still to write: 'Dear All . . . '

'About bloody time,' said Helen. 'They'll be worried sick.'

I ignored her, staring at the window, and then out of the window as the train emerged from a tunnel into bright sunlight. I kept my eyes open for a man standing on a roof feeding birds from a saucepan. No luck. Instead a great flock of birds rose off a building in a scary startled leap, spreading out into the sky like a soundless explosion. I watched them until they were out of sight before I looked back into the carriage.

There she was, opening her mouth to heckle me some more. I stared at her, stared her down until she turned away blushing. I looked closely at her for the first time. It wasn't Helen. Her hair was wrong for a start, hennaed to a reddish sheen and close cropped at the sides – when had she last worn it like that? And her face. This girl's face wasn't very expressive, there was a solidity to it like that of the corpse in my fantasy. And something familiar about that abashed expression, something of myself there.

The tube lurched, faces appeared at the windows as it slowed down to a stop. The crowd on the platform squeezed into the carriage and it was quickly transformed, becoming hot, loud and airless, the inside of a radio, full of voices complaining about the weather and the crowds and the lateness of the train.

A woman sitting next to me was delivering a rapid monologue to the nodding sympathy-murmuring companion who stood in front of her.

'Now she's gone she's gone is how I look at it you see, it's the best thing that could have happened. She was a burden to herself poor lamb in any case, but now she's in a happier place thank goodness, not that she was unhappy. And to me of course, yes of course, she was a burden to me as well.'

I felt qualified to contribute some lines of my own. 'I only knew him for six days,' I could have said. 'He was very quiet about it, he put a brave face on it. I only knew him for six days and he didn't even look that ill.'

Easy enough to play a part. It was a question of choosing one to adopt, as in those competitions: complete this sentence in the most apt and amusing way. Complete it in the right *voice*.

'Move down the bloody aisle!' A man crushed against the door was getting annoyed. Some faces turned and a few people shuffled forward.

'There's no call for that kind of language,' said the monologue deliverer, as her companion moved away.

'No,' I agreed, since she was looking at me now, 'there's no need for it.'

'But it is rather crowded. I find that it always is at this time of day.'

'Yes,' I said, 'no room to move. When all you ask is a little privacy.'

'What have you been doing?' Oblivious or indifferent to my hints, she was looking at the stick leaning on my seat.

'I've been to the doctor's,' I said.

She looked at me blankly for a moment, then smiled and said 'No dear, I meant what have you done to your leg?'

I looked at her. I am not spontaneous, there is too long a gap between thought and speech. This means that I will never be either a natural wit or scrupulously truthful. I looked at her and said, 'Shrinking limb disease.'

'Whatever's that?'

'Anaesthbomia. It's simply the shrinking of one or more limbs.' I held out my arms. 'You may notice that my left arm is slightly shorter than my right.'

'My goodness, just the slightest yes. Astonishing. Anass- what?'

'Anaesthbomia. Anaesth- as in anaesthetic; bomia, b-o-m-i-a. Greek for limb. It means something like sleepy limb. That's what the papers call it, sleepy limb disease. You'll have seen it in the papers.'

'Astonishing.'

'Very rare of course. Tends to lead to paralysis eventually. Life goes on, more or less, but the limbs, what's left of them, are paralysed. Movement is impossible, things tend to grind to a halt.'

'How awful.'

'Not a pleasant prospect. You can imagine the problems I'm sure.'

'Of course.'

'Incidentally, why did you ask?' A taken-aback silence. 'Because

116

really,' I went on, 'although I'm content to talk even to strangers, I don't feel I owe them my life story.'

We had arrived. I wriggled out of the train, Simon the liar again, trying to straighten out my attitude to honesty.

I felt conspicuous as I limped towards Helen's house, past a line of net-curtained windows. On my right a railway embankment, where tangles of weeds fought cans and rusty prams. Kids were playing football in the road, using parked cars as goals. They had to pause as I walked slowly by, and I felt their eyes on me. What was I going to say? My uneven pace became more eager as I approached the house, but I felt at a loss for words, nostalgic for a plan. Honesty, dishonesty, self-pity, silence, all casting their conflicting votes.

My finger on the bell, I hesitated. This is where I am at the end of the summer, I am at the front door of Helen's house. The front door, that is the key, everything is still ahead of me, but now I feel at least that I have reached the door.

I rang the bell, ready to present my flowers, eloquently, and then I was confronted by a girl I didn't recognise. She had an even, doll-like face, neatly framed by a mousy bob. 'Hello,' I said, 'maybe I've got the wrong house. Does Helen live here?'

'Oh yes,' she said, with a bright smile at my confusion. She turned. 'A friend for you, Helen', she shouted up the stairs, and then she disappeared into a room off the hall.

I came in and shut the door and was standing in the hall taking my coat off when Helen came down the stairs towards me. Her legs were bare beneath a very short skirt and her hair, in loose copper curls, fell freely around her face. 'Hello my love,' she said.

'I could watch you coming down the stairs all day long.'

She laughed and ran back up them and came down again, slowly, in a parody of a tv model. She evoked no memories as she did this, she was too present to evoke any memories.

I met her a couple of steps up and we kissed. Her hands on my waist seemed to touch my skin directly, as if my shirt wasn't there.

'You're looking beautiful', I said.

'Thank you.' She scrutinised me. 'You look like you just got up.'

117

'It's been a busy day already.'

She shook her head. 'And your poor leg. You mustn't overdo it.'

'I'm planning a lazy afternoon.'

'Me too,' she said, 'funnily enough.' And then, taking her hands from her waist and raising them to her temples, 'Do you like my hair?'

I felt it, soft and curly next to her cheek. 'Yes,' I said, 'it keeps changing, doesn't it? Listen,' still standing next to her, two stairs up, 'listen. I want to change too.' A pause as our eyes met. 'I don't know what to say about last time. Except sorry. I mean I was just trying to needle you, it was petty, and unforgivable basically. I'm very sorry.'

She shook her head. 'I forgive you that,' she said. 'What was *un*forgivable was not telling me about the hospital. That was unforgivable.' But her smile was the one I remembered, brief and full, her eyes didn't leave mine, and she asked for no explanations. 'Are the freesias for me or what?'

'For you,' I said. 'A token.'

She took me upstairs to show me her room, where the sun shone through the open windows on to a ransacked mess of clothes and books and bits of paper, scattered tapes and odd items of makeup. A lipstick lying in one cup of a bra, like a sea-creature revealed in its shell.

'I was just clearing up', she said, 'when you arrived. Sit down, don't sit on the typewriter.'

I sat and watched her gathering clothes by the armful and putting them in drawers. Makeup made a colourful pile in front of the mirror, and papers, apparently indiscriminately, went into the bin. I gathered some of the books and put them on shelves while she made the bed, and before long the floor was visible again and there was enough space to move around.

'Sorry about that,' she said, 'I don't know where it all came from. It keeps accumulating until I can't breathe.'

'That's just what I used to think, that we should have had aqualungs.'

'I'm going to reform. Tracy nags me too.'

'Tracy answered the door?'

'Yes. I'm living with her and a girl called Frances. Trace is out of work too, and permanently fraught.' She laughed. 'You'll like her.'

This was Helen I was talking to, with a new haircut, bare legs, and a loose green sweatshirt. Last time I saw her, it was through the filter of a plan: she was the provider of cues, the antagonist and the victim. She was only alive for me in my need to move closer, and to touch her. Now I looked at her and found her presence almost intimidating, as if we had just met and the sexual tension between us was unexplored. Now I listened to her talking and nodded and responded, and was aware of her presence. I felt the distance between us, and knew that most of it could be crossed. There was so much to say.

After more preliminaries she asked me about the biopsy, and I told her quickly what Dr Hunt had told me that morning. She looked more upset than I had been. Her sudden, urgent hug seemed to be trying to squeeze the illness out of me. 'I'm sorry, Simon,' she said. 'I thought, you know, I thought that's what this was leading up to. Oh, shit.' This because she was crying. I told her about the eighty per cent success rate and said, uselessly, that there was nothing for her to be sorry about.

'Yes,' she said, looking at me and still hugging me, 'well, I don't know. What's the next move?'

Her body against mine. It was hard to keep my mind on being ill. 'I think tomorrow. I think tomorrow they'll have more to tell me. I mean they'll give me dates.'

She let go of me. 'I'm sorry,' she said again, as if for letting go. Then quickly, 'Let's have lunch.'

In the kitchen, grating cheese onto runny eggs in a frying pan, she was self-conscious. I saw her finding something to say, to fill the silence, then turning to me with an accusing pout.

'When can I have the meal you promised me?'

'Did I promise you a meal?'

'You know you did,' she said, waving the grater at me and dropping long shreds of cheese on the floor. 'You made me a salad and you said you'd make me a proper meal next time. It was a very nice salad, mind you.'

119

She tried to sandwich the tomato and cheese into the omelette, and tipped most of it out into the frying pan.

'Fuck!' A pent up vehemence in the word. 'Don't you want to do this, love?'

'Too many cooks . . .'

'Smug sod. So when are you going to cook for me?'

'I will soon, it's a good idea. God knows what I'll be doing. I don't know my plans yet, or their plans yet, that's the problem.'

Tracy came in while we were eating, draped in a white dressing-gown now, with a sleepy sort of smile on her face.

'I thought what I needed was a bath,' she said, 'to start the day off on the right foot.' She put the kettle on the boil. 'And a cup of tea.'

When she had gone Helen looked at me meaningfully. 'She's looking you over,' she said.

'I expect you've told her all about me?'

'No no,' she said. 'I've just dropped tantalising hints. That's all we do, we drop hints at each other. Like you and I used to.'

Helen has a mannerism, she draws her fingers across her forehead, as if tracing lines over the smooth skin. Under her hand her eyes weighed me. A curl in the corner of her smile?

She laughed abruptly when the armchair exhaled a creaky groan as I sank into it. She started talking about it, telling me how she had bought it in a junkshop. She described the shop and the owner for me, and the problems in transporting the chair to her room. Mr Pock did not enter my mind then, only entered it in retrospect, and then only as an embarrassing oddity, like a performer still in costume after the end of a show. I was preoccupied by Helen's increasingly nervous manner, rather than by her words. The mystique around cancer makes it hard to set aside, even when it is not the most important thing. I felt myself retreating back to a voyeur's position, watching her talk to me, telling me the story of the chair. It was a story she had told before, and it came out glibly enough. I watched myself sitting in the chair, fingering a hole in its floral covering. 'Imagine,' she was saying, 'how many people have sat there.' Did they fill it out better than me?' And speak more ably? Why was I moving apart from her again, instead of responding to her nervousness?

She had stopped talking and was looking me. 'We haven't said anything yet.'

'No.'

'What are you thinking about?' She had been standing to tell the story, now she sat on the arm of the chair and asked the question Vincent had asked: 'Are you worrying about what the doctor said?'

I accepted this diversion from her first question, and tried to be honest about it. 'I don't think I am worrying. I think that's part of the problem, I don't think I am.'

Misinterpreted: 'Why won't you tell me? Sweetheart, be nice to yourself, don't keep it to yourself.'

'I'm trying to talk to you, you see that's the hard part.'

'Talk.'

'You said when you visited me that we weren't strangers, but we are in a way. I think I understand you leaving me, that's o.k. now, but I'm still having problems with the present. I mean for instance the problems of talking to people. As for cancer, I haven't even begun, I'm still waiting to react to that. It doesn't seem the most important thing at all.' The unclarifying images: 'Maybe in the biopsy they took out something extra, a sly cut around the chest or something. I mean they took something away, because some feeling is missing, I'm sure I should be feeling more than I am.'

'Aren't you feeling anything?' The nervous laugh again. 'You look like you're feeling something.'

The codes: 'Confused, that's all. I get scared by the view from a train, a colourful bunch of flowers makes me unhappy. There are memories and associations that take me by surprise.'

Then something odd happened. She was sitting on the arm of the chair, beside and above me, one of her arms across the back of the chair, very close to me, almost slipping towards me, when I started trembling again. As if I was feverish, not just my hands shaking but my whole body, so that it didn't stop even when I pressed my palms flat against my thighs. This violent trembling, within the circle of her arm. She stood up and moved away with her back to

121

me to the cluttered desk where she picked something up or moved something while she changed the subject, still with her back to me.

I didn't hear what she said. I watched her. Her head bent over whatever it was on the desk, curls hiding her face. Her long legs bare. A sweatshirt on, as if she had just been dancing. She moved over to the window now, and I felt less confused as she moved away, calmer, because a clear-cut choice had neatly emerged and I saw my chance at last to shape events. Pity, affection, guilt; I was certain, suddenly, that some misleading combination of feelings had made her ready to have me back. All I had to do was stand up and go to her. Serendipity: the moment we had arrived at was right for a tearful reunion. We would both find reassurance in decisive movements, in the dishonest faces we would show each other. All I had to do was stand up and go to her.

I settled deeper into the armchair, and carefully chose my words and my tone.

'Life hasn't lived up to my hopes,' I said. 'I wanted a significant life, my problem was a deep-seated conviction that I *deserved* a significant life. All of it suddenly falls apart, I mean the centre of the whole thing goes and the rest is just ragged and, and this is comical, I blame everyone but myself. Recriminations, resentment, like a rained-off fireworks display, lots of damp bangers and failed explosions. I want to slot back into place now. It's more than putting the phone back on the hook and answering letters, I want to build bridges and rediscover relationships and talk to people. Or else it's futile, isn't it. So please don't be nervous, because things are better than they were. Do you remember what you said, in the flat, about the walls closing in? Well it's true, they were, they were closing in and I was in some kind of paralysis, just watching them. I know there are new restrictions now, but I still feel I've got more room to move than I've had all summer. More room to move and much more to say.'

Helen had turned round about halfway through this and sat down at the desk. She nodded at the last comment, her expression sceptical. 'So what *are* you going to do?'

'I don't know that yet. I'm not saying I know that.'

'Well it sounds all right, I mean you sound confident, but I don't know how much sense it makes.'

'Well even that's an improvement, if it sounds all right.'

There was a knock on the door and Tracy came in, refreshed after her bath, in a smart black dress. She looked around the cleaned-up room.

'You're honoured,' she said to me.

'Come in,' said Helen, 'be introduced. Tracy, Simon; Simon, Tracy.'

'I just came in to see if you wanted a coffee or something.'

We didn't. 'Are you going out tonight?' I said.

'No,' she said, 'unless you're asking?'

'I meant the dress.'

'Oh the dress. It's just a dress.'

'I always know what mood she's in by what she's wearing,' said Helen.

'No coffee?' said Tracy.

'No thanks,' I said.

She left, and we heard her going downstairs to the kitchen.

'She seems bored,' I said.

'Yes,' said Helen. 'I expect that's the only reason she wanted you to ask her out.'

'Don't start matchmaking.'

Tracy: another on my list of names. The cast is growing. Tracy: unemployed, depressed, eccentric according to Helen. Doll-like face, mousy bob, conventionally pretty. Sub-plot character?

'When I first went into hospital,' I said, 'I couldn't believe there were so many people who were ill. The thing is now, I can't believe there are so many people, period. So many people to know or not to know. I've been bouncing off people all summer, not talking to anyone.'

'I know about that,' said Helen. 'Big big mistake. I was like that, but only for about a week, then suddenly over two days I phoned everyone I knew, everyone I could think of until the next month, May and June, was dotted all over with dates. It's what you should have done.'

'Mmm-hm. Yes. I mean yes, I admit it, it just wasn't on the cards at the time. Three months though, three months is long enough to pause, isn't it?'

Cross-legged on the chair at the desk, Helen nodded. 'Too too too long.' She looked at her bare legs. 'I'll get changed,' she said, 'and we'll have a walk. Let's go out tonight, I know a good place we can go.'

'There's a good place?'

'There's *always* a good place.'

We had a small candlelit table in a corner by a window. Outside the window, nothing, only darkness. There was no tension left. We spent the afternoon walking around where Helen lives, around a park and through a cemetery, finishing outside the local pub, drinking and composing epitaphs. 'No thanks,' said Tracy, when we asked her to come to the restaurant. 'I'll leave you two to get to know each other.' A weight of words in me now, enough words to challenge Steve. Words are my latest secret. I began as our main courses arrived.

'What throws me is that there *were* times when nothing else mattered, weren't there?'

'Of course there were,' said Helen, taking a forkful of lamb and rice. 'Lots of times.'

'I knew there were.'

'Not enough of them for you though.'

'I got hooked on us.'

She waved her empty fork at me, 'Eat, don't just talk, this is nothing new. I started feeling I was alone, even with you there. I remember thinking one day I may *have* to be alone, relatives dead, friends gone, strangers around me. I mean I could really frighten myself. Don't rush it, I was thinking, one day it may be for real.'

I began to extract the spine from my fish. 'I'm trying to think how I could let that happen. I'm trying to follow up clues.'

'It wasn't just me being unhappy then, Sherlock. You weren't very happy either as far as I could tell. That was the really stupid part.'

'But you made me feel whole, that was the point.'

'Two people, Simon, we were two people, not one. I felt diminished.'

'When you went I felt like you'd taken me with you. I was in the flat but the flat was empty.'

I bared my teeth at her as I took a bone from my mouth, and she bared hers, gratuitously, before she answered. 'Don't start over-dramatising. I took away nothing. And don't drink that, that's mine.'

'Another bottle?'

'No.'

'Another bottle.'

'All right then. How's the mullet?'

'Fine.'

'I took away nothing, how could I, I lost as much as you did. Keep that in mind.' She leant forward, her cream dress criss-crossed by shadows in the candle-light, her hair changing colour: red, copper, auburn. Her face slim, slightly heavy around the chin, big eyes, a redhead's pale complexion. Jealousy came and went. She said, 'Your tunnel vision fucked us both up.'

'And the lamb?'

'Delicious.'

'It fucked me up more than you.'

'Well you would say that, wouldn't you? Being so self-regarding.'

'Because when you'd gone, *still* nothing else mattered. I looked around and none of it meant anything. That was the real problem. I was like an immigrant in a new world but what I was forgetting was that the world was exactly the same, only I had changed. I was looking for ways of explaining it and interpreting it, as if it was all in Chinese and I couldn't take a step without a phrase-book.' The bottle arrived, and our glasses were refilled. 'That's been my excuse, that you and everybody changed, so it's not my fault that I don't understand.'

In the window my face was reflected, intent, as if it was a third person, listening to my words.

'Do you remember,' I said, 'of course you remember, how I'd play with ingredients? I'd be after the perfect recipe. We'd have a meal somewhere that was good, but I'd insist that it wasn't quite right, so later I'd be juggling with ingredients to make it right. There'd always be something missing. Good wasn't good enough. That's what I mean, the perfect recipe, that's what I've been after.'

'Don't wave your cutlery at me, love. That's another excuse, that's just an *excuse* for being unhappy because you know you can't find a perfect recipe.'

'Well I'm not being unreasonable anymore. Just a good enough one, I mean what you've got there looks good enough, it's not hard to find. Just a way of living that feels right. Can I try yours?'

'My way of living?'

'Your lamb.'

She gave me a forkful. 'When you find this way of living that feels right, I mean if it's not too elusive, will you let me know please?'

'You al*ready* know, that's the secret. The secret is that you don't realise, you just go ahead and do it, do the recipe, keep throwing the right things in.'

'Will you stop that? Stop telling me about myself please? You're being self-regarding again, you see, at the drop of a hat. It's easy for you to think it's easy for me. Part of the *problem* is that you think it's easy for everyone else. You shut people out like that. Don't grin when you're being criticised, give me some fucking mullet.'

'What's happened to your language?' I held out a forkful and she guided my hand towards her mouth, but I stopped it. 'People keep tempting me to say 'fuck off' too. It's very difficult. It's another problem. Do you know what I keep thinking of? Love. I mean that's got to come into it, hasn't it? A primary ingredient.'

I made to move my hand but she held it, the tines of the fork at her lips. 'Simon, I don't like where this is heading.'

'What, you want it somewhere else? Your ear?'

'Shut up, you know what I mean. I'm not going to talk about love with you.'

'Am I wrong or is that the title of a song? You're wrong as it happens, it's not heading there at all. If you don't want to talk about love, all right, but it's your problem.'

She smiled now, mostly with relief. 'Well, all right then.' She finally took the fish. 'Love is an ingredient. But what's your hurry?

You would take days to put those recipes together, the more you were interested the longer it took. You have to expect it to take a while to work out a way of life.'

'This has taken months already.'

'A way of life, Simon.'

'Not a way of life, a way of living.'

'So? So be patient. I mean don't do nothing either. What I'm doing advising, I don't know.' Fingers across the forehead again. 'This is all a bit late, isn't it? I couldn't say anything when I really needed to talk to you. I've spent the summer not thinking about things. Now that I'm with you I don't want you to think I'm your foul weather friend, only around because . . . because of a crisis.'

'I don't think that. I think we're back on speaking terms for the first time since well before you left. Just at the right time. Just in time.'

'Well, what have we actually decided?'

'I know *all* my relationships broke down, and not just the one with you, although that one first and foremost. So the building programme begins. I'm an inner city that needs revitalising. There's that. And I've decided, and this is important, I've decided that not understanding isn't important. It's o.k. not to understand.'

'All this just to get that straight?'

'No, *more* than that. Don't you feel better? All this to feel better.'

'I've decided nothing. Except all this should have been said months ago.'

'Can I have the last word?'

'Yes.'

'You're right.'

So the words achieved nothing, beyond the pleasure of using them, exchanging them with another person, with no sense of evasion or prevarication or duelling. Only a sense of heading in a common direction. Eventually a tentative feeling, an optimistic bubble of a feeling that sometime, conceivably, we might talk our way to the truth.

Leaning over the table towards each other we kissed, as if to congratulate each other on deciding almost nothing, a smiling kiss, chins hot over the guttering candle. Plenty of words left, I was thinking. There is still a world to be said.

On the tube on the way home, in the notepad diary I had taken to carrying around, I finally wrote the letter to my family. It was concise and uncluttered, in the style of my letter to Helen, but with an attempt at reassurance (eighty per cent success rate), nonchalance (had a meal with Helen tonight), and humour (there's this beautiful night-nurse). I couldn't resist ending though on, for them, an enigmatic note: My consolation is that *finally*, although the summer is nearly over, I am learning Chinese.

DAPPLE

October 24th
(Evening)

This must be the weekend at the beginning of the story. I wish it was halfway through. Here I am in the present tense, and I want to jump off into the future. I wish I could flick through and reach next year's entries, and skip all the stuff in between.

This morning, after a shower, the thick wet towel round my neck like a collar as I walked back to my room . . .

No, this won't work. I'm just beginning to realise – not my mistakes, that was the easy part, the ball and chain of memory is nothing compared to the pipe and the fat bag of the drip feed – I'm just beginning to realise that this second story is not as light or as bright as I would like it to be. Any other feeling is just optimism. 'More room to move than I've had all summer.' Easily said. There's not much room to move when you're plugged in to a drip feed which is feeding you a litre of poison.

So I'll exercise the strictly limited powers of the diarist and jump out of the hallway between bathroom and bedroom, jump ahead to the park, the October park, wishing all the time that I might overshoot and accidentally jump clear into next year.

October, the sky a dark grey with scrapings of blue. Just enough sun to justify my reminding you of its presence, lurking behind the clouds, raising the temperature now and then for a few moments before being hidden again. A cool breeze without the legs to be called a wind, but working up to it, jogging round the park in no hurry, working up to it. Not much flesh on view, Summer clothes replaced or bolstered by sweaters and warm coats. Colours are fading: green to khaki, yellow to rufous brown. The leaves are dying, I can smell them burning. All in all, my favourite time of year.

I was standing outside the playground by the hedge watching children spinning the roundabout, hanging on to it and running frantically in a circle around it, jumping on as it gathered squealing momentum. Some of their parents stood nearby, complaining about the shortness of the days and speculating about what kind of winter to expect. A boy tumbled off as the roundabout picked up speed, and he rolled over and over across the concrete almost, comically, to his parents' feet. Nothing happened. They picked him up and quieted his crying, watched him run back to his friends, and then they rejoined the conversation. Why not a circle of sand around the roundabout, for safety's sake? Do you remember last year's snow? The boy's friends admired his grazed elbow, and allowed him to sit on the roundabout while they pushed it round again.

I walked off the path, past the cordoned-off cricket pitch, and sat down in an expanse of grass, then lay down in it, exploiting an interlude of sun while the breeze exercised in some other corner of the park. One hand under my head, the other by my side, fingers teasing the grass. A sense of the curve of the earth beneath me, fitting smoothly into the curve of my spine. For a few fragile moments, a serene, equinoctial sense of poise. Then the clouds returned, the breeze returned, and I took my cane and left.

On the way back to my flat I bought food for my family, a bagful at the butcher's, a chat with him about prices, another bagful at the greengrocer's. 'Don't make it anything special,' mum said on the phone, 'you can't afford it.' 'Cheese sandwiches,' I told her. While I was studying the vegetables, I realised that a man was staring at me. I looked at him and saw that his gaze was on my cane, its rich varnish and its silver top. No N.H.S. stick this, but a dandy's cane, bought from a smiling lady in an antique shop in Tufnell Park. He raised his eyes to meet mine.

'Very nice,' he said. 'Is it affectation or does it have a practical purpose?'

I picked up an avocado. 'Pure affectation.'

'Really?'

'No, I'm lying. In fact I hurt my leg skiing.'

'In the autumn?'

'These days you can ski anytime.'

'You mean on a dry slope.'

'No, I don't.'

'Well where?'

'Just off Oxford Street.' I put down the avocado and showed him my hand. 'Look, no more trembling.'

We stood there for a moment with my hand held out ambiguously between us, and then he shrugged and turned away.

Awkwardly back to the flat, the two bags in one hand, the cane in the other, one light load, one heavy. I waited for the lights to change. Awkwardness, I was thinking, is still my problem. Over the road. I'm talking about a tightrope: I spend my life walking fine lines. Up the stairs, slowly. Standing outside my door, looking for a key, I remembered my months'-old resolution, to think about Mondays, to think about the future and make plans. That's what has depressed me, that to understand my mistakes doesn't help; I have given up plans, resolutions, deceptions, formulae and rash promises, but it doesn't help to have given them up. There is still awkwardness, and awkwardness is expressed in hostility. I understand the thin man better than I did. Why be civil to every stranger? My list of names is not as long or as arbitrary as I thought it might be. So many people. What do you say to so many people? I stood there outside the door trying to find the key, not wanting to put down bags and cane, searching through my pockets, Stupid, where did you put it?, and then dropped both bags and cane, dropped them rather than put them down, and finally found the key in an inside pocket of my jacket. The neighbour across the landing opened her door at the sound of the crash. 'Are you all right?' 'Fine thanks.' Just stupid.

The secret is to stop being stupid, then it will be all right. I've finished with this diary already. What else is there to say?

October 25th

The limits and latitudes of preparing lunch were entirely fulfilling.

131

An apricot stuffing, with fried onions, breadcrumbs and an egg, moulded between my palms into sweet-smelling cubes, like dice. Vegetables, peeled, chopped and piled, synchronised with the slow-cooking lamb smeared in olive oil, garlic and rosemary. Maybe I do have the patience to be a chef. The oven's gust of hot air, an ohhh of appreciation.

Last night improved. I talked to Helen to say I'd be staying in for the evening, and her voice reminded me that hostility to strangers is a long-term problem, not an urgent one. Some concern, some badgering, bad jokes about Tracy's disappointment and Agnes's jealously. Look, I said, it's hard to broach anything over a bowl of vomit. Go on, she said, broach, broach. I was left in a good mood, feeling I was learning smooth talking, the art of talking without disengagement between thought and words. Then a quiet evening in. The last queasiness had gone by that time so I had a big meal, read a little, watched some tv. Regaining the knack of being alone.

Back to today. 'It's lovely,' said Mum, 'but how can you afford it?' 'Magnificent!' said Dad. From his excitement you'd think I'd given birth to the animal before I cooked it. 'Say thank you,' said Mum as I passed Sammy his plate. 'He's my brother, I don't say thank you.' 'Oh yes you do,' she said. But he'd seen my expression and he was unpersuadable. 'I don't have to say thank you,' he insisted. 'He's my brother.'

Self-consciousness only set in once during the meal, when we were talking about the future. We were doing quite well – I sounded interested, Dad made suggestions which Mum qualified, we were doing quite well until we became self-conscious about something, or about an accumulation of things, and then suddenly we had nothing to say, as we remembered that the future was not something to be taken for granted. Only Sammy takes it for granted, he treats it like one of the user-friendly computers they have at school, waiting for a programme to be put in. His faith is in a pleasant myth, as mine was when my aunt was alive and working up far-fetched tales of her adventures. The sounds of eating seemed to get louder, and Mum played with her empty glass as if she was about to perform a quick miracle and drink from it. We all plot personal histories into the future, as if we were the omnipotent narrators of our own stories. It's a bad habit we grow into. I wanted to explain: 'It's all right, I'm not plotting, I'm taking a day-to-day approach.' But I just sat there, dumb as mutton.

Dad eventually responded to this silence, heroically considering his usual inclinations after a Sunday lunch. Rubbing his ear in his wisest manner he said, 'Glory be to God for dappled things. We'll visit your park.' A beaming, would-be infectious smile, because he was so pleased with his idea. 'I'd like to see some trees.'

'Oh, da-ad,' said Sam.

But he was right, it was a good idea. We felt like a family as we left the flat, on a family outing.

'What a shame Steven's not here,' said Mum.

'Christmas,' said Dad firmly. 'The three of them will be here for Christmas. *Wait* till you see your nephew. Isn't he lovely, Sam?'

'He's very small.'

We had another archetypal autumn day, crisp and bright and, just for Dad, dappled. The wind was throwing its weight around, gusting and bullying the leaves.

'Look!' said Sam. 'Look how high it is!'

Twice as high as the tallest tree – a kite, a yellow lozenge straining at two taut lines which quivered like the strings of an instrument. The man controlling it, leaning slightly away from its tug, brought it swooping down towards him like a trained bird. The dog at his heels jumped as if he had shouted an order at it and raced after the kite, barking dementedly. This was a really dumb dog, chasing backwards and forwards, head straining upwards in a kind of dynamic hypnosis, and the man knew it was dumb and teased it, bringing the kite sailing down close, having it hovering just out of reach, and then making it soar away towards the clouds with a mocking wind-rattle and a flourish of the tail.

'He mustn't tease it,' said Mum, shaking her head.

We walked on under the trees, Sam running ahead and kicking leaves into the air, Mum and Dad praising the weather and talking about winter, me thinking about the dog dancing up and down under the kite, making a fool of itself. Sam came charging back towards us, brown as the leaves he was kicking, and without pausing I dropped my cane and picked him up, whirled him round and kissed him before he could protest, and then set him down again wobbling between our parents.

A NOTE ON THE AUTHOR

Mark Illis was born in Blackheath in 1963, and educated at University College, London, and the University of East Anglia. His first published short story was a runner-up for the Whitbread Prize for Young Writers; subsequent stories have been published in the *London Review of Books* and *Fiction Magazine*. Mark Illis lives in London, and is working on a second novel.